John Langhorne, William Collins

Poetical Works

With memoirs of the author, and observations on his genius and writings

John Langhorne, William Collins

Poetical Works
With memoirs of the author, and observations on his genius and writings

ISBN/EAN: 9783337093396

Printed in Europe, USA, Canada, Australia, Japan

Cover: Foto ©Andreas Hilbeck / pixelio.de

More available books at **www.hansebooks.com**

T. Stothard del. R.A.   J. Neagle sc.

ECLOGUE III.

Oft as she went, she backward turn'd her View,
And bade that **Crook** *and bleating Flock adieu?*

Published by Cadell & Davies Strand Sep.ʳ 1.1797.

THE

POETICAL WORKS

OF

MR. WILLIAM COLLINS:

WITH A

PREFATORY ESSAY,

BY MRS. BARBAULD.

———————

LONDON:

RINTED FOR T. CADELL, JUN. AND W. DAVIES,
IN THE STRAND,

BY W. FLINT, OLD BAILEY.

═══

1802.

POETICAL WORKS

OF

Mr. WILLIAM COLLINS.

THE different species of Poetry may be reduced under two comprehensive classes. The first includes all in which the charms of verse are made use of, to illustrate subjects which in their own nature are affecting or interesting. Such are Didactic and Dramatic compositions. Such is the Epic, where a story, a series of adventures, carries the reader on through the impulse of curiosity, and loses not its interest intirely even if translated into Prose. Such are descriptions of natural objects, where the mind recognizes with pleasure the forms and colouring it

a

admires in the various scenes and productions of the visible world. Such is, also, that moral painting of men and manners, that spontaneously approves itself to the spirit of observation, and the moral sense, that more or less are implanted in the breast of every man. Hence the Essays and Epistles of POPE have been popular among all that read. A lively representation of the *passions*, particularly those of Love, Terror, and Pity, commands the attention even of those who are but indifferent judges of the vehicle in which it may be conveyed. The other class consists of what may be called pure Poetry, or Poetry in the abstract. It is conversant with an imaginary world, peopled with beings of its own creation. It deals in splendid imagery, bold fiction, and allegorical personages. It is necessarily obscure to a certain degree; because, having to do chiefly with ideas generated within the mind, it cannot be at all comperhended by any whose intellect has not been exercised in similar contemplations ; while the conceptions of the Poet (often highly metaphysical) are rendered still more remote from common apprehension by the figurative phrase in which they are clothed. All that is properly *Lyric Poetry* is of this kind. It depends for effect on the harmony of the verse, which must be modulated with the nicest care; and on a felicity of expression, rather than a fullness of thought. An Epic Poem may be compared to a piece of massy plate finely wrought; it is intrinsically valuable, though its value is much increased by the work bestowed upon it. An Ode, like a delicate piece of silver filligree, receives in a manner all its value from the art and curiosity of the workmanship. Hence Lyric Poetry will very seldom bear translation, which is a kind of melting-down of a Poem, and reducing it to the sterling value of the matter contained in it. Who can read the greatest part of the Odes of HORACE in any translation that has yet appeared? and who, but a native of France, reads, what a native of France reads with rapture, the Odes of JEAN BAPTISTE ROUSSEAU?—Nor can this species of

Poetry, though most answering to SHAKESPEAR's definition, as it gives *to airy nothing a local habitation and a name*, ever be popular. The *substratum*, if I may so express myself, or subject matter, which every composition must have, is, in a Poem of this kind, so extremely slender, that it requires not only art, but a certain artifice of construction, to work it up into a beautiful piece; and to judge of or relish such a composition requires a practised ear, and a taste formed by elegant reading. MOLIERE, it is said, used to submit his *Comedies* to the criticism of an old woman; but the most beautiful *Ode* will only please those who, by being long conversant with the best models of Poetry in a polished age, have acquired a scientific and perhaps, in some degree, a factitious taste.

COLLINS, amongst our English Authors, has cultivated the Lyric Muse with peculiar felicity; his works are small in bulk, but highly finished; and have deservedly gained him a respectable rank amongst our minor Poets. His characteristics are tenderness, tinged with melancholy, beautiful imagery, a fondness for allegory and abstract ideas, purity and chasteness of sentiment, and an exquisite ear for harmony. In his endeavours to embody the fleeting forms of mind, and clothe them with correspondent imagery, he is not unfrequently obscure; but even when obscure, the reader, who possesses congenial feelings, is not ill pleased to find his faculties put upon the stretch in the search of those sublime ideas, which are apt, from their shadowy nature, to elude the grasp of the mind.

COLLINS has written but little, and is said, probably with truth, to have been inclined to indolence; but it is likewise true that the man of fine imagination who draws his productions from the stores of his own mind, ought to have large allowance made before this accusation is fixed upon him. A real Poet must always appear indolent to the man of the world. The alacrity and method of business is not to be expected in his occupation. His mind works in silence, and exhausts itself with the various emotions which it cherishes, while to a common eye it appears fixed in stupid apathy. The Poet requires long intervals of ease and leisure; his imagination should be fed with novelty, and his ear soothed by praise. But it was not the fortune of COLLINS to meet with that notice which his productions have since obtained; and after he had published his beautiful Odes, indignant and disappointed at the slowness of the sale, he is said to have burnt the remaining copies with his own hands. His end was unhappy; his mind, abandoned to inaction, preyed upon itself, and he fell into that malady most humiliating to a being possessed of rational powers.

The Epistle to Sir THOMAS HANMER seems to have been the first of our author's productions. As the subject is historical, rather than fanciful, it has less of the peculiar manner of COLLINS than any other of his Poems. In a slight, but neatly executed sketch, he traces the state of the Drama through the writers of other countries; and with a partiality,

in which the other nations of Europe seem almost
to acquiesce, gives the palm to the Englishman's
idol, SHAKESPEAR, after whom,

> " No second growth the western isle could bear,
>
> " At once exhausted with too rich a year."

It is probable that our Poet, who was then a student at the university, knew nothing at that time of
MASSINGER; otherwise, when he distinguishes
SHAKESPEAR from FLETCHER, by the strength
and masculine turn of his Drama, he could not
have omitted one who came so near him in those
characteristic qualities. It is remarkable, that in
this piece, the plan which has since been carried
into execution through the spirit and liberality of
Mr. BOYDELL, that of a gallery of paintings to illustrate the pieces of our great Dramatist, is here first
proposed to the public. The subjects are particularly pointed out, Coriolanus reluctantly yielding
to the intreaties of his wife and mother,

> " Rage grasps the sword, while pity melts the eyes."

And, Antony, pronouncing the funeral oration over
the dead body of Julius Cæsar;

" Still as they press he calls on all around ;

" Lifts the torn robe, and points the bleeding

    " wound."

It were to be wished that all the scenes which have
been transferred to the canvass had been selected
with as much judgment. It is not every scene that
may be found in SHAKESPEAR, which illustrates
SHAKESPEAR.

In 1742, while COLLINS was still a student at
Magdalen College, he published his ORIENTAL, or,
as they were first intitled, PERSIAN ECLOGUES.
Sensible of the triteness of common Pastoral, which
had become almost proverbial, the author has endeavoured to throw interest and variety into this elegant species of composition, by introducing the manners, and especially the appropriate scenery of other
countries. The attempt was laudable, and the effect
happy. The Oriental Eclogues have not indeed at-
tained equal popularity with the Delias and Stre-

phons of the Arcadian school, but they have always stood high in the opinion of real judges, and have opened sources of new and striking imagery which succeeding Poets have often availed themselves of. The passions of men are uniform ; but, modified by the influence of climate, government, manners, and local circumstance, and accompanied with the various tints which employ the pencil of a landscape painter, they present an inexhaustible variety, from the song of SOLOMON breathing of cassia, myrrh, and cinnamon, to the Gentle Shepherd of RAMSAY, whose damsels carry their milking pails through the frost and snows of their less genial, but not less pastoral country. The province of Pastoral may in this way be enlarged to take in all the beautiful and all the grand appearances of Nature, which observation or reading may have brought the Poet acquainted with ; he may sport in the vast savannahs of America ; he may regale his shepherds with the bread-fruit of Otaheite, or sadden them

with the prospect of an impending eruption of Mount
Vesuvius.

The Eclogues are four in number, corresponding
to the four periods of morning, noon, evening, and
midnight. SELIM, or the SHEPHERD'S MORAL,
is the least interesting of the number. It has nothing dramatic in its structure, and the two similes
with which it is adorned are more quaint than beautiful. It is, however, calculated to please by the
purity and sweetness of its moral ideas, and serves,
as it were, to prepare and put the mind in tune for
virtuous sympathy with the feelings of shepherds.
The personification of Chastity,

"————— of all afraid,

" Distrusting all, a wise suspicious maid ;

" But man the most ————"
is remarkably happy.

HASSAN, or the CAMEL-DRIVER, stands upon
a ground of superior merit. There is a peculiar
strength of painting in the opening of the Poem.
The horror of a boundless desart, arid and sultry,

the intense beams of noon, the absence of all vestige
of vegetation, the undulating ocean of sand swept
by the rising whirlwind, present a scenery of gloomy
grandeur strictly appropriate to the country. A
single group appears upon the canvass, composed of
laden camels, so emphatically called in the East the
ships of the desert, pursuing their painful march
through a cloud of dust, and the driver Hassan,
with his single cruise of water, and fan made of
feathers, who is represented striking his breast with
his hand, according to the eastern expression of
strong emotion, before he begins his complaint.
The scene is highly finished, and shows what advantage might be gained to this kind of Poetry, by studying the more picturesque features of nature. This
piece is a monodrame, but the apostrophe to the
camels, and the introduction of the speech of Hassan's mistress, give it sufficient dramatic effect. The
danger incurred in these desarts from poisonous
reptiles and wild beasts is strikingly impressed:

"What if the lion in his rage I meet!

"Oft in the dust I view his printed feet."

The images in the two following lines seem to be borrowed from the 5th chapter of Matthew,

"The lily, Peace, outshines the silver store,

"And life is dearer than the golden ore."

There is a prettiness in the prayer of Zara, that the blasts of the desart might be weak as her rejected sighs, which is unworthy of the rest. COLLINS had a fine imagination, but he did not possess the language of passion. There seems also a small impropriety in Hassan's bearing the cruise of water himself, when he was master of laden camels.

The subject of the next Eclogue is truly pastoral. A young shepherdess making garlands of such flowers as, though they are the product of our gardens only, are known to grow wild in many parts of Persia, is discovered by Abbas the Great, sultan of that country, who falls in love with her, and leads her to his palace. Filled with awe, no less than pleasure, she complies with the wishes of the monarch ; but, like Proserpine in the valley of Enna, looks back with fond regret on the peaceful scenes of her happy life ;

" Oft as she went, she turn'd her backward view,

" And bade that crook and bleating flock adieu."

A pretty incident is added, that she makes an annual visit to the place of her former habitation, and persuades her royal lover to accompany her in a rural festival, in which they lay aside the pomp of the court for the garb and simple fare of the surrounding shepherds. As the narrative is put into the mouth of another Georgian maiden, who relates it among her companions, there should have been some return to her at the close of the piece, without which we are apt to forget that Emyra and not the Poet is the narrator.

AGIB AND SECANDER is in every respect the most finished of these Pastorals. It is the only one which is in dialogue. It is full of lively description, and mixes the sweetness of the Pastoral with the

keener sensations of the Drama or the Epic. The
opening is natural, and immediately interests us in
the fate of the speakers. The subject is new, interesting, and strictly belonging to the life of shepherds in those countries, which are unhappily ex-
posed to the incursions of bordering tribes of free-
booters. Two Circassian shepherds flying from the
sudden attack of a horde of Tartars, pursue their
journey by midnight for some time, " Where wildering fear and desperate sorrow led ;" after a
while, one of them, exhausted by the length of
the way, intreats the other to stop, on which a dialogue ensues, descriptive of the miseries of the inhabitants. At length they descry the approach of the
enemy.

" —— loud along the vale was heard

" A shriller shriek, and nearer fires appear'd."
This naturally puts an end to the dialogue ; they
rise and continue their flight. Circassia has the reputation of producing the most beautiful women of
the east. This gives the Poet a favorable opportu-

nity of contrasting the soft scenes of innocence, love
and pleasure, with the affecting ones of wasted harvests, citron groves destroyed, villages in flames, and
all the destructive ravages of predatory war. The
two following lines are uncommonly musical, and
have an indescribable charm in their versification,

" In vain she boasts her fairest of the fair,

" Their eyes' blue languish and their golden hair."

He adds

" Those hairs the Tartar's cruel hand shall rend."
With equal truth of penciling does he mark " the
villain Arab prowling for his prey."

Some feeble or unmeaning epithets might be
pointed out in this and in the other Eclogues; and
other marks may be perceived of a juvenile poet; but
on the whole, they may be considered as spirited
sketches of a new kind of Pastoral, which is susceptible of unlimited variety and improvement.

The reputation of COLLINS is chiefly built upon
his Odes. These were published in the year 1746.
They are intitled ODES DESCRIPTIVE AND ALLE-

GORICAL.   Allegorical they certainly are, so far as that term may be applied to the personification of abstract ideas, though *figurative* would perhaps have been a more proper term : but they do not seem to have an equal claim to the epithet *descriptive*; by which we generally understand a delineation of some portion of real nature. Few of the Odes of COLLINS are of this cast, which indeed does not belong so properly to the nature of the Ode ; but they are in the high spirit of pure Poetry. Their beginning is commonly abrupt and bold; often a spirited apostrophe :

" Thou to whom the world unknown

" With all its shadowy shapes is shewn !"
Sometimes it is in the interrogative ;

" *Who shall awake the Spartan fife ?*"

The language is highly figurative, sometimes obscure ! the measure is various ; the versification in general easy and flowing, and in many passages wrought up to all the harmony the English language is capable of exhibiting.

The first of these compositions, TO PITY, is
chiefly remarkable for the sweetness and tenderness
congenial to the subject. Pity is represented as
being sent into the world to bind the wounds and
sooth the sorrows of man,

> " When first Distress with dagger keen
> " Broke forth to waste his destin'd scene."

The *eyes of dewy light* is an expression peculiarly
happy; but the personification of *Distress* does not
seem equally accurate, since Distress is commonly
used for the sensation felt by the person afflicted,
not for misfortune itself. The mention of OT-
WAY, born as well as COLLINS, near the Arun,
probably suggested to his melancholy and indignant
mind an analogy in their fates, which he has forborne
to express. They both of them were the objects
of pity, from that circumstance in which a liberal
mind would least wish to become so, pecuniary
distress. The idea of building a temple to Pity, on
the walls of which should be painted a variety of

b

tragic subjects, might, if the Poet had pleased, have enabled him to lengthen his ode, by enriching it with sketches to any extent.

The ODE TO FEAR is one of the finest in the collection.   Nothing can be more spirited than the opening, which at once introduces the mind to all those undefined terrors which wait upon " the world unknown." The break in the fifth line, *Ah, Fear ! ah frantic Fear ! I see, I see thee near !* has the happiest effect on the ear and on the mind. The hurried step, the haggard eye, the withering power of Fear, are all highly characteristic. *Danger* with gigantic limbs enjoying the midnight storm, and sleeping on a loose precipice; and the *ravening brood of Fate who lap the blood of sorrow*, are finely imagined. It is difficult to keep intirely separate the active and passive qualities of allegorical personages: difficult to say whether such a being as Fear should be the agent in inspiring, or the victim agitated by the passion. In this Ode the latter idea prevails, for Fear appears in the character of a nymph pursued, like DRYDEN's Honoria, by the ravening brood of Fate. She is distracted by the ghastly train conjured up by Danger, and hunted through the world without being suffered to take repose; yet this idea is somewhat departed from, when the Poet endeavours to *propitiate* Fear by offering her as a suitable abode, *the cell where Rape and Murder dwell;* or a cave, whence she may hear *the cries of drowning seamen.* She then becomes the power who delights in inflicting fear. But perhaps the reader is an enemy to his own gratification, who investigates the attributes of these shadowy beings with too nice and curious an eye. In his reference to the goblins of Midsummer eve, the Poet shews that disposition to take advantage of the traditionary superstitions of his country, which he afterwards indulged more fully in his Ode on the Highland Superstition, a piece he did not live to finish. The division of this Ode into Epode and Antistrophe is no advantage to it. The change of measure is so violent from the Lyric to the Elegiac, that in fact they make two different Poems; and the terms themselves not being supported, as among the ancients, by any adaptation of musical accompaniments, are in our Poetry totally unmeaning. The complimentary valediction, so often imitated from MILTON, *And I, O Fear, will dwell with thee*, is in this instance but a compliment; for however a man might be content to have his days tinged with the soft influence of a penseroso-melancholy; he could not, for any reward, wish to subject himself habitually to the distracting emotions of such a passion as Fear.

The ODE TO SIMPLICITY is chiefly distinguished by a smoothness and uniformity of melody, adapted to the sober nature of the subject. It chiefly insists on the power of Simplicity in touching the heart, and its necessary connection with Liberty: the latter, though a sentiment we have early imbibed, is probably imaginary. The Poet is obliged

to include the Augustan age of writers under the
votaries of Simplicity, and how few were the Poets
whom the Romans had to boast of before that pe-
riod? Where COLLINS is not sustained by richness
of Poetry, his sentiments will be found to be trite.

ON THE POETICAL CHARACTER. This is one
of the most difficult and perhaps least satisfac-
tory of the Odes. It begins with an ingenious com-
parison drawn from SPENSER. As the girdle of
Florimel, though apparently within the reach of all,
would not fit any but the virtuous fair destined to
wear it, so the girdle of Fancy, the magic cestus
of poetic powers, can only be worn by him whom
Nature has cast in the mould of true genius. So
far is apt and intelligible; but the Poet afterwards,
actuated, as it should seem, by a vague desire of
exalting his favorite occupation, rather than by any
clear and distinct ideas, goes on to say how this
cestus was produced. His allegory here is neither
luminous nor decent. The Supreme Being, he tells
us, being in a *diviner mood than usual*, retired with

Fancy, having long been wooed by her, (from whom
retired? for nothing was yet created,) and placed
her on his throne, sitting with her there alone; in
the mean time music was heard from behind the
veil; the sun, signified by *the rich-hair'd youth of*
morn, and all the visible creation, started into being; and as the work of creation went forward, this
magic web, the cestus, was woven: and who, after
this account, he adds, will now dare to assert his
claim to it?

It is difficult to reduce to any thing like a meaning this strange and by no means reverential fiction
concerning the Divine Being. Probably the obscure
idea that floated in the mind of the Author was
this, that true Poetry being a representation of Nature, must have its archetype in those ideas of the
Supreme Mind, which originally gave birth to Nature; and therefore, that no one should attempt it
without being conversant with the fair and beautiful, the true and perfect, both in moral ideas, *the*
shadowy tribes of mind, and the productions of the

material world. Some of the separate images are good, as, *ecstatic wonder, listening the deep applauding thunder;* and the description of the residence of MILTON approaches the sublime; though the quaint expression of *his evening ear* is not to be commended*. The Author concludes with expressing his despair of fulfilling, or seeing fulfilled by any future Poet, that high idea of the poetical character which he has been impressing on the mind.

The ODE ON THE DEATH of COLONEL ROSS, is in perfect contrast with the former. It is flowing, tender, and touches all the springs of sympathetic sorrow. Every sweet allusion which can sooth the hero fallen in the bed of honor, is here conjured up with a masterly hand! and when, from the patriotic ideas of freedom, honour, and just vengeance over the enemies of our country, the Poet by a sudden change in the movement reverts to the situation of the mourning and desolated friend, un-

---

* The *tarsol, by whose eyes those of Truth were made,* is the *ger-hawk* or *falcon; tarsol* or *tiercelet,* being an old term in falconry, used to express the males of that species of hawk.

able to forget the real sorrows of life in the contem-
plation of shadowy glories,

> " If yet in Sorrow's distant eye,
> " Expos'd and pale thou see'st him lie,
> " Wild war insulting near;"

the soul is struck, and acknowledges the force of
Nature above the power of lofty figures or swelling
sentiment. The WILLIAM mentioned in the poem
is the hero of Culloden, then a favorite with the
people. It is not improbable that in this Ode
the Author had in view the popular song of Hosier's
Ghost. The beautiful little dirge which follows
this piece, bears the same relation to it, which an
elegant vignette does to an engraving of full size.

The maxim of HORACE, *Ut pictura poesis*, may
be strictly applied to the first stanza of the ODE
TO MERCY; for the figures and attitudes are de-
lineated so perfectly, that a painter has nothing left
to do but to transfer it to the canvass. Valour,
under the figure of an armed youth, sits grasping
his spear with a threatening gesture. Mercy, in

the character of a bride, seated beside him is employed in covering his sword with wreaths of flowers; and by her blandishments endeavours to get his spear out of his hand.

This Ode, as well as the former, seems to have been written just after the rebellion of 1745, and was probably intended to move pity, possibly to express sympathy towards the unhappy victims of an ill-judged and abortive attempt to raise the fortunes of a fallen race. He seems to refer to this transient interruption of the peace of these kingdoms, in another piece, where he invokes Concord to return to the *ravaged* shores of Britain.

To LIBERTY. The opening of this spirited Ode rouses the mind susceptible of patriotic feelings, as with the sound of a trumpet.

" *Who shall awake the Spartan fife,*

" *And call in solemn sounds to life—*

The subject of the Poem is similar to that of THOMSON's long, and to say the truth, rather heavy, composition, which bears the same title.

Its object is to give a free and rapid sketch of the various states which in different ages have possessed this inestimable blessing. Having called up interrogatively the shades of Sparta and Athens, the gigantic Republic of Rome is represented under the original and striking figure of a huge statue, which after having stood the wonder of ages, is pushed from its base, and broken to pieces at length by the rude conquerors of the North. In this place the imitative harmony of the following line is much to be admired,

   " *With heaviest sound a giant statue fell.*"*

The various free states which arose out of the ruins, as Venice, Florence, &c. are fragments of this great mass. They are denoted by little characteristic circumstances, historical, or picturesque, which give truth and life to the description, *sunny Florence; the willow'd meads of Holland, to whom the stork is dear; he who weds in the Adriatic his green-*

---

* Perhaps, however, the hint of the image was caught from that in Nebuchadnezzar's dream.

hair'd bride; jealous Pisa's olive shade; the daring archer, &c. The remainder of the piece is taken up in complimenting Britain upon possessing in the fullest manner the affection of the Goddess :

" For thou hast made her vales thy lov'd, thy last
        abode."

COLLINS has here taken advantage of a tradition, that Britain was formerly connected with the continent; and of another, less known, that in the time of the Druids there existed in Britain, a temple sacred to Liberty. *The wide wild storm even Nature's self confounding*, by which our island is supposed to have been separated, is described with great force and beauty of language. It may be observed, however, that the Author is obliged to MILTON's Comus, for some of his images; *the green navel of our isle.*

" *Within the navel of this hideous wood.*" Comus.

" And see like gems her laughing train,
" The little isles on every side,"
" That like to rich and various gems inlay
" **The** unadorned **bosom** of the **deep.**" Comus.

The hyacinthine locks of the Spartans, though an expression very classic, has, to an English reader, more of sound than of sense it; especially if referred, as it is here to the colour; yet the magic of numbers is such that the passage cannot be read without pleasure, and the allusion to the custom the Spartans had of arranging their hair before a battle, is just and happy.

Beautiful as is this Ode, the philosophic reader will find much to object to. The ideas of Liberty referring to ancient states, are formed upon those splendid notions which are imbibed in early youth, and are little applicable to the real and practical principles of just legislation. The practice of slavery alone completely destroys, in all those states who used it, all pretence to the blessings of fair and equal government; and there exists no country where the stern regulations of power entered, more than at Sparta, into every scene of private life. The parent could not there exercise the sacred and inalienable right of education; nor the husband enjoy his home. And with regard to religious liberty, so dear to every ingenuous and in-quiring mind, it was not even thought of in the Gre-cian States. As to Rome, the Author has fallen into the anachronism common to the admirers of antiquity, of confounding the times of the republic with those of the empire; in order, by blending the glories of each, to delight the imagination with an æra more free than the later, more splendid than the earlier periods of its history; for surely *that* Rome which was overthrown by the *northern sons of spoil*, had no claim to draw down the tears of Freedom at her fall.

ODE TO EVENING. As the English language will bear verse without rhyme in the ten-syllable Heroic measure, and even possesses many pieces of that kind which are admired for the harmony of their cadence, it has been the opinion of many that blank verse might also be extended to our Lyric measures, and several attempts have been made to realize this idea, amongst which the *Ode to Evening*

is undoubtedly the most beautiful. It has more of
description than any other of the Poems of COL-
LINS, and the whole of it is highly finished. The
imitative harmony of the following lines will
scarcely escape the reader,

" ———————————— the weak-eyed bat,

" With short shrill shriek flits by on leathern wing;"
nor the exquisite description of the gradual approach of Evening,

" And hears their simple bell, and marks o'er all

" Their dewy fingers draw

" Their gradual dusky veil."

His propensity to *the pensive pleasures sweet*,
which pervades all his Poems, appears with much
grace in this address to Evening, where it peculiarly suits the sober and quiet character of that season. But notwithstanding its superior merit considered as a Poem, in the chief object of its construction, this Ode will probably be considered rather as
a literary curiosity than as a successful pattern of a
new made of versification. The imagination indeed

is gratified, but the ear is disappointed; nor is this merely the effect of custom. So long as our verse is constructed chiefly with Iambics, particularly in the close of the line, the absence of rhyme will appear a defect; but Lyric measures might be formed composed of dactyls and anapæsts, which would probably sustain themselves without this ornament, by some thought so Gothic; the only objection to this, and it is to be feared an insuperable one, is, that our language does not naturally run into these measures, and the genius of a language cannot be forced. Those who think no practice can have the stamp of taste which has not the sanction of the ancients, will continue to inveigh against rhyme; writers, studious of novelty, will, from time to time, make attempts to do without it; but we may venture to pronounce it far from probable, that the mode in which the great masters of English versification, from POPE to DARWIN, have charmed the readers of successive generations, should be discovered to the offspring of tasteless caprice, or the blind compliance with unmeaning custom. It is moreover a fact, which those who have tried it will bear witness to, that the necessity of labouring the line, and turning the expressions frequently in the mind, is favorable to excellence; and that, whatever might be presumed to the contrary, a thought is oftener condensed than dilated by the necessity of putting it into rhyme. Our common blank verse is so extremely easy to compose, that it tempts a young author to negligence. The art of versification is as essential to the nature of Poetry as beauty of thought; and however difficult it may be to bind in rhyme the unwilling phrase, the Poet should remember that he cannot free himself from a chain, but by abandoning an ornament.

To PEACE. In reading the Author before us, our attention cannot but be attracted by the frequent recurrence of those subjects which indicate a gentleness of temper, and a quick sensibility to the distresses of his fellow men. COLLINS did not use the liberal breath of Poetry to fan those flames

which consume and destroy mankind ; Peace, Mercy,
Pity, these are the themes he delights to dress and
adorn with all his pomp of imagery ; and his gentle
spirit seems to have been wounded with the contem-
plation of the miseries of his race.   The image of
Peace escaping to the skies, and just saving her hair
from the furious grasp of her enemy, is appropriate
and beautiful,

"——————————————tergoque fugaci

" *Imminet, et crinem sparsum cervicibus adflat.*"
This Ode was probably written during the war of the
Austrian succession.

THE MANNERS.   That COLLINS was more
fond of abstract and metaphysical ideas than of the
busy haunts of common life, his works sufficiently
evince.   It must, therefore, have been in some
moment of disgust against the usual train of his
ideas, that he professes himself desirous to aban-
don the philosophic porch for the walks of life ; and
speculation, for wit and humour.   We may reason-

ably conclude, however, that with wit and humour as well as with speculation, his acquaintance was formed through books ; and that when he speaks of studying the Manners, he had only laid down his Plato to take up Gil Blas. The scintillations of wit are ingeniously alluded to by,

" The jewels in his crisped hair,

" ⸻ placed each other's beams to share."

The remark that the name of *humour* is known only to Britain's favoured isle, is calculated to mislead; since surely no one will pretend that the *thing* is peculiar to our own country; and it is of little importance that the terms do not exactly correspond in different languages. LE SAGE should not have been characterized by the story of *Blanche*, which, though beautiful, is not in his peculiar style of excellence, and has more to do with the high passions than with *Manners.* Indeed the subject isn ot particularly proper for an Ode, and, though not devoid of merit, this is by no means one of his most striking pieces.

THE PASSIONS. The connection of Music with Poetry, and their united power over the Passions, has been a favorite theme of authors. DRYDEN, who had a musical ear, and POPE who had none, have both written Odes for St. Cecilia's day. To try his strength with these great masters, was an exertion worthy of the ambition, and not above the powers of COLLINS. This Ode to the Passions may be considered as the happiest production of his pen. His art is the more to be admired, as he has not, like his predecessors, taken advantage of a story for the basis of his piece ; but has raised it solely on an allegorical fiction of his own. The Passions, who had often crowded round the cell of Music, while she sung in early Greece, being once upon a time more than usually affected, and raised into a kind of ecstacy, snatched her instrument which hung upon the surrounding myrtles, and produced, each of them, a strain suitable to the peculiar expres-

sion of his character. The Passions are thus enumerated in the beautiful lines of Pope,

" Love, Hope, and Joy, fair Pleasure's smiling

" train,

" Hate, Fear, and Grief, the family of Pain."
This division is not exactly followed. Hate is given
under the different modifications of Anger and Revenge. Fear, with that of Despair. Jealousy is
introduced; a passion compounded of many others.
Grief is, with the happiest effect, softened into Melancholy. Joy is preceded by Cheerfulness; and
Love, all-powerful Love, is only mentioned inciden-
tally. The reader may perhaps expect from the
frame of the piece that an appropriate instrument
should be found for every passion, as in the ingenious paper of ADDISON, in which characters are
resembled to musical instruments. This however is
not the case. To some of the passions no particular instrument is assigned. Anger and Joy
have two; and the horn, though with " an altered
tone" is common to Melancholy and Cheerfulness.

The aim of the Poet was rather to describe them by their manner of playing, than by a circumstance which, if extended to every one, might have given rather a formal air to the Poem, and allied it more to wit than to fancy.   In the order in which they are brought forward, the sole view seems to have been that they should relieve one another; Melancholy is followed by Cheerfulness; the song of Hope is broken off by Revenge; and *his* movements are contrasted by those of Pity.   It may perhaps be asked, why Fear is set in the front of the contest; he is described, however, very characteristically. He does not properly play, he *lays his* " *hand,* bewilder'd, amid the " chords," and is startled at the sound he has himself produced.   Anger *sweeps the lyre in one rude clash.*   It **is** rather a violent fiction to make Despair play at all.   So deadening a sensation hardly leaves room for any exertion.   The next is truly enchanting.   It begins with a sprightly apostrophe,

" *But thou, O Hope ! with eyes so fair,*

Her song, for she sings as well as plays, is prolong-
ed at every close, and *the soft responsive voice*, at
which " *Hope enchanted smiled, and waved her golden*
" *hair*" is conceived in the happiest spirit of allegorical fancy.   The break in the next line has a fine
effect ; it seems to show Revenge entering like a stern
conqueror through a breach : the doubling drum, the
sword thrown in thunder down, and the strained
eyeball bursting from the head, mark the character
with its proper strength ; and we have already observed how well it is contrasted with that of Pity.
Jealousy is more feebly drawn, but Melancholy is
in his softest, mellowest style of colouring.   She is
placed apart from the rest, surrounded with such
appropriate scenery as a pensive mind naturally
delights in ;

      " With eyes uprais'd, as one inspir'd,

      " Pale Melancholy sat retir'd."

And her notes die away into silence, by soft and
imperceptible gradations, **in** a cadence much finer
than the *dying dying fall* of Pope executed in the

same key. Cheerfulness is exhibited with a lively group about her, the action is animated, and gives much of the dramatic to the piece. The Satyrs are *peeping* from *their alleys green ; brown Exercise* rejoices ; and *Sport leaps up and seizes his beechen spear.* Is it because the nature of man is less formed for rapture, than for moderate exhilaration, that when the Poet endeavours to rise from Cheerfulness to Joy, the images are less distinct, and the effect less forcible ? The unaccountable exclusion of Love from the trial has already been noticed ; but surely, if he was mentioned at all, it should have been as a principal, and not introduced dancing like a Bacchanal in the train of Joy. This is what could hardly have been expected from the delicate and sentimental COLLINS. But whether from the shyness of his disposition, or some early disgust, or from whatever cause, certain it is that he has shown himself rather unfriendly to the passion to which the greater part of Poets have largely sacrificed. In his Pastorals there is as little of it as is well consistent with the nature of the composition, and in another place he refers to it only in the way of complaint.

"Love, only love, her forceless numbers mean."

It is a test of merit, and not a symptom of defect in this Ode, as has been surmised by some critic, that its beauties are brought out by recitation. No composition in the language is more admirably adapted to display with effect the different modula-tions of impassioned sentiment and imitative har-mony, and it is remarkable that this is effected not by a studious adaptation of particular measures to the expression of different passions, for the same measure is often used for opposite passions; but by that skilful mixture of them, by those graceful cadences and judicious breaks, and sounds convey-ing the tone of feeling to which the ear of a Poet is his best guide. The allegory is simply this, that the *art* of music supplies the instruments, but that the Passions alone can make them speak to the heart; and the piece concludes with lamenting the

dissolution of that union which is said to have sub-
sisted in ancient times between Poetry and Music.
Of the wonderful effects of this union, every one
perhaps is not prepared to affirm with our Author,
" 'Tis said, and I *believe* the tale;" but every person of taste must lament its divorce from *sense*, and
regret, that while the English language offers to the
composers of music such productions as the pre-
ceding for the basis of their exertions, the degra-
dation of the public taste obliges them to prefer,
for their charming structure of sweet sounds, the
slang of Newgate, the vulgarisms of the province,
or the lisping prattle of the nursery.

ODE ON THE DEATH OF THOMSON. This
piece is tender and plaintive; the allusion to the
Æolian harp, the *dashing oar* suspended to bid his
gentle spirit rest, the gradual fading of the scenery
as night approaches, are pleasing and picturesque
circumstances. But there is no propriety in calling
THOMSON a Druid or a pilgrim, characters totally
foreign to his own. To the sanguinary and super-

stitious Druid, whose rites were wrapped up in mystery, it was peculiarly improper to compare a Poet whose religion was simple as truth, sublime as nature, and liberal as the spirit of philosophy. *Nature's child* is a proper epithet, but why *meek Nature's child.* In short there is nothing characteristic of the Author he wished to commemorate, nor does there seem to be any local acquaintance with the scenery, for the church of Richmond is not white, nor a spire, nor can it be seen from the river; and as to the monument, erected in the last verse to this great Poet, it must be looked upon in the light of a prophecy which is not yet fulfilled.

There remain two or three smaller Poems, among which the dirge in Cymbeline deserves to be noticed, as perfectly corresponding with the delicacy and sweetness of the play for which it was written as an accompaniment.

To the Poems which have usually been published as the works of Collins, is now first added, An ODE ON THE POPULAR SUPERSTITIONS OF THE

HIGHLANDS OF SCOTLAND, which was read by the Reverend Dr. CARLYLE on the 19th of April, 1784, at the Royal Society of Edinburgh. It was inscribed to Mr. JOHN HOME, and fell into the hands of Dr. CARLYLE, among the papers of a deceased friend, where it lay unregarded till a hint, given by Dr. JOHNSON, in his life of COLLINS, of the existence of such a Poem, revived the remembrance of it, and after diligent search it was found in the hand-writing of the Author. It seems to have been the first rough draught of the Poem; it was written in the year 1749, and probably the Author, who died in 1756, never enjoyed spirits sufficient to finish it. Several hemistichs and words left blank have been supplied by Dr. CARLYLE; and the fifth, and half of the sixth stanza, by Dr. MACKENZIE, with such art, that if it were not for the inverted commas, by which his lines are distinguished, the garment would appear without a seam. The *cordial youth* mentioned in the second stanza was a Mr. BARROW,

who had been taken prisoner with Mr. HOME,
(both of them volunteers at the battle of Falkirk),
and then resided at Winchester, where Mr. COL-
LINS and Mr. HOME then were.

The purport of this Ode is to recommend to the
Poet of Scotland the popular superstitions of his
country, as peculiarly proper for works of imagination. These are enumerated with equal taste
and knowledge of the subject. The imagination of
COLLINS was apt to kindle at whatever bore the
impress of the strange, the wild, and especially the
supernatural : no wonder, therefore, he was struck
with the tales of the second sight, the elf-shot ar-
rows, the island of pigmies, &c. in which the northern part of our island abounds. The information
is chiefly taken from MARTIN's account of St.
Kilda. It does not appear that COLLINS was ever
in Scotland. The horror which those possessed of
the second sight are said to feel often at the visions
they see, is advantageously touched upon:

" How they whose sight such dreary dreams en-

" gross,

" With their own visions oft astonish'd droop;

" When o'er the wat'ry strath or quaggy moss

" **They** see the gliding ghosts unbodied troop.

" They know what spirit brews the stormful day,

" And heartless oft, like moody madness stare,

" To see the phantom train their secret work

" prepare."

The seventh and eighth stanzas which describe a peasant drowned by the wrath of the Kelpie, are particularly beautiful. The apparition of the pale and bloated corpse " with drooping willows drest," standing before his wife, reminds us of a similar pathetic passage in Ceyx and Alcyone*,

" Then he perhaps, with moist and wat'ry hand,

" Shall fondly seem to press her shudd'ring cheek,

---

* Luridus, exangui similis, sine vestibus ullis,
Conjugis ante torum miseræ stetit : uda videtur
Barba viri, madidisque gravis fluere unda capillis.

Metam. xi.

" And with his blue swoln face before her stand,

   " And shudd'ring cold these piteous accents

      " speak."*

The island of St. Kilda is marked by a negative circumstance highly descriptive,

" *Nor ever vernal bee was heard to murmur there.*"

But notwithstanding these and other striking passages, this Ode is far from possessing the spirit and pathos of the Ode to Fear. Many of these prodigies, woven into a story, would contribute strongly to the effect, but here the Author speaks, and the Author has told us at the setting out that he does not believe them. It is, however, a Poem well worth recovering, and does credit to COLLINS, though it is not one of the few on which his reputation will more particularly rest.

The reader, after thus going through the productions of COLLINS, must have formed his opinion

---

* The blue swoln face is much superior to the *luridus* of the Latin Poet.

of the powers of the writer. He will be acknow-
ledged to possess imagination, sweetness, bold and
figurative language. His numbers dwell upon the
ear, and easily fix themselves in the memory. His
vein of sentiment is by turns tender and lofty, always tinged with a degree of melancholy, but not
possessing any claim to originality. *His* originality
consists in his manner; in the highly figurative garb
in which he clothes abstract ideas; in the felicity
of his expressions; and his skill in embodying
ideal creations. He had much of the mysticism of
Poetry, and sometimes became obscure, by aiming
at impressions stronger than he had clear and well-
defined ideas to support. Had his life been pro-
longed, and with life had he enjoyed that ease and
health which is necessary for the undisturbed exercise of the faculties, he would probably have
risen far above most of his contemporaries. As it
was, he did not enjoy much of the public favor;

but posterity has done him justice, and assigned
him an honorable rank among those of our Poets
who are more distinguished by excellence than
by bulk.

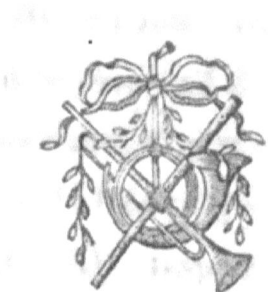

ORIENTAL

ECLOGUES.

B

ECLOGUE I.

SELIM; or, THE SHEPHERD's MORAL.

SCENE, A VALLEY NEAR BAGDAT.

TIME, THE MORNING.

YE Persian maids! attend your poet's lays,

And hear how shepherds pass their golden days.

Not all are blest, whom Fortune's hand sustains

With wealth in courts; nor all that haunt the plains:

Well may your hearts believe the truths I tell;

'Tis virtue makes the bliss where'er we dwell.

Thus Selim sung, by sacred Truth inspir'd;

Nor praise, but such as Truth bestow'd, desir'd:

Wise in himself, his meaning songs convey'd

Informing morals to the shepherd maid;

Or taught the swains that surest bliss to find,

What groves nor streams bestow, a virtuous mind.

When sweet and blushing, like a virgin bride,

The radiant morn resum'd her orient pride;

When wanton gales along the vallies play,

Breathe on each flower, and bear their sweets away;

By Tigris' wandring waves he sat, and sung

This useful lesson for the fair and young.

Ye Persian dames, he said, to you belong,

Well may they please, the morals of my song:

No fairer maids, I trust, than you are found,

Grac'd with soft arts, the peopled world around!

The morn that lights you, to your loves supplies

Each gentler ray delicious to your eyes:

For you those flowers her fragrant hands bestow,

And yours the love that kings delight to know

Yet think not these, all beauteous as they **are,**

The best kind blessings Heaven can grant the fair!

Who trust alone in beauty's feeble ray,

Boast but the worth Bassora's pearls display;

Drawn from the deep, we own their surface bright,

But, dark within, they drink no lustrous light:

Such are the maids, and such the charms they boast,

By sense unaided, or to virtue lost.

Self-flattering sex! your hearts believe in vain,

That love shall blind, when once he fires the swain;

Or hope a lover by your faults to win,

As spots on ermin beautify the skin:

Who seeks secure to rule, be first her care

Each softer virtue that adorns the fair;

Each tender passion man delights to find,

The lov'd perfections of a female mind!

Blest were the days when Wisdom held her reign,

And shepherds sought her on the silent plain;

With Truth she wedded in the secret grove,

Immortal Truth! and daughters bless'd their love.

O haste, fair maids! ye Virtues, come away,

Sweet Peace and Plenty lead you on your way!

The balmy shrub for you shall love our shore,

By Ind excell'd or Araby no more.

Lost to our fields, for so the Fates ordain,

The dear deserters shall return again.

Come thou, whose thoughts as limpid springs are clear,

To lead the train, sweet Modesty! appear:

Here make thy court amidst our rural scene,

And shepherd-girls shall own thee for their queen.

With thee be Chastity, of all afraid,

Distrusting all, a wise, suspicious maid;

But man the most—not more the mountain doe

Holds the swift falcon for her deadly foe.

Cold is her breast, like flowers that drink the dew;

A silken veil conceals her from the view.

No wild desires amidst thy train be known,

But Faith, whose heart is fix'd on one alone:

Desponding Meekness, with her down-cast eyes,

And friendly Pity, full of tender sighs:

And Love, the last: by these your hearts approve,

These are the virtues that must lead to love.

Thus sung the swain; and ancient legends say,

The maids of Bagdat verified the lay:

Dear to the plains, the Virtues came along,

The shepherds lov'd, and Selim bless'd his song.

ECLOGUE II.

HASSAN; or, THE CAMEL-DRIVER.

SCENE, THE DESERT.

TIME, MID-DAY.

IN silent horror o'er the boundless waste

The driver Hassan with his camels past:

One cruise of water on his back he bore,

And his light scrip contain'd a scanty store;

A fan of painted feathers in his hand,

To guard his shaded face from scorching sand.

The sultry sun had gain'd the middle sky,

And not a tree, and not an herb was nigh;

The beasts, with pain, their dusty way pursue,

Shrill roar'd the winds, and dreary was the view!

With desperate sorrow wild, th' affrighted man

Thrice sigh'd, thrice struck his breast, and thus began:

   " Sad was the hour, and luckless was the day,

   " When first from Schiraz' walls I bent my way!"

   Ah! little thought I of the blasting wind,

The thirst or pinching hunger that I find!

Bethink thee, Hassan, where shall thirst assuage,

When fails this cruise, his unrelenting rage?

Soon shall this scrip its precious load resign!

Then what but tears and hunger shall be thine?

   Ye mute companions of my toils, that bear

In all my griefs a more than equal share!

Here, where no springs in murmurs break away,

Or moss-crown'd fountains mitigate the day,

In vain ye hope the dear delights to know,

Which plains more blest, or verdant vales bestow:

Here rocks alone, and tasteless sands are found,

And faint and sickly winds for ever howl around.

    " Sad was the hour, and luckless was the day,

    " When first from Schiraz' walls I bent my way !"

    Curst be the gold and silver which persuade

Weak men to follow far fatiguing trade !

The lily peace outshines the silver store,

And life is dearer than the golden ore:

Yet money tempts us o'er the desert brown,

To every distant mart and wealthy town.

Full oft we tempt the land, and oft the sea;

And are we only yet repaid by thee?

Ah ! why was ruin so attractive made,

Or why **fond man** so easily betray'd ?

Why heed we not, while mad we haste along,

The gentle voice of Peace, or Pleasure's song?

Or wherefore think the flowery mountain's side,

The fountain's murmurs, and the valley's pride,

Why think we these less pleasing to behold,

Than dreary deserts, if they lead to gold?

   " Sad was the hour, and luckless was the day,

   " When first from Schiraz' walls I bent my way!"

Oh cease, my fears!—all frantic as I go,

When thought creates unnumber'd scenes of woe;

What if the lion in his rage I meet!—

Oft in the dust I view his printed feet;

And, fearful! oft, when day's declining light

Yields her pale empire to the mourner night,

By hunger rous'd, he scours the groaning plain

Gaunt wolves and sullen tigers in his train:

Before them Death with shrieks directs their way,

Fills the wild yell, and leads them to their prey.

"Sad was the hour, and luckless was the day,

"When first from Schiraz' walls I bent my way!"

At that dread hour the silent asp shall creep,

If aught of rest I find, upon my sleep:

Or some swoln serpent twist his scales around,

And wake to anguish with a burning wound.

Thrice happy they, the wise contented poor,

From lust of wealth, and dread of death secure!

They tempt no deserts, and no griefs they find;

Peace rules the day where reason rules the mind. —

"Sad was the hour, and luckless was the day,

"When first from Schiraz' walls I bent my way!"

O hapless youth! for she thy love hath won,

The tender Zara will be most undone!

Big swell'd my heart, and own'd the powerful maid,

When fast she dropt her tears, as thus she said:

" Farewell the youth whom sighs could not detain,

" Whom Zara's breaking heart implor'd in vain!

" Yet as thou goest may every blast arise

" Weak, and unfelt as these rejected sighs!

" Safe o'er the wild, no perils may'st thou see,

" No griefs endure, nor weep, false youth, like me!"

Oh let me safely to the fair return,

Say, with a kiss, she must not, shall not mourn;

Oh! let me teach my heart to lose its fears,

Recall'd by Wisdom's voice, and Zara's tears.

He said, and call'd on Heaven to bless the day,

When back to Schiraz' walls he bent his way.

ECLOGUE III.

ABRA; or, THE GEORGIAN SULTANA.

SCENE, A FOREST.

TIME, THE EVENING.

IN Georgia's land, where Tefflis' towers are seen,
In distant view along the level green,
While evening dews enrich the glittering glade,
And the tall forests cast a longer shade,
What time 'tis sweet o'er fields of rice to stray,
Or scent the breathing maize at setting day;
Amidst the maids of Zagen's peaceful grove,
Emyra sung the pleasing cares of love.

Of Abra first began the tender strain,

Who led her youth with flocks upon the plain:

At morn she came her willing flocks to lead,

Where lilies rear them in the watery mead;

From early dawn the live-long hours she told,

'Till late at silent eve she penn'd the fold.

Deep in the grove, beneath the secret shade,

A various wreath of odorous flowers she made:

*Gay-motley'd pinks and sweet jonquils she chose,

The violet blue that on the moss-bank grows;

All sweet to sense, the flaunting rose was there:

The finish'd chaplet well adorn'd her hair.

Great Abbas chanc'd that fated morn to stray,

By love conducted from the chase away;

* These flowers are found in very great abundance in some
of the provinces of Persia.

Among the vocal vales he heard her song,

And sought the vales and echoing groves among:

At length he found, and **wooed** the rural maid;

She knew the monarch, and with fear obey'd.

" Be every youth like royal Abbas mov'd,

" And every Georgian maid like Abra lov'd."

The royal lover bore her from the plain;

Yet still her crook and bleating flock remain:

Oft, as she went, she backward turn'd her view,

And bade that crook and bleating flock adieu.

Fair, happy maid! to other scenes remove,

To richer scenes of golden power and love!

Go, leave the simple pipe, and shepherd's strain;

With love delight thee, and with Abbas reign.

c

" Be every youth like royal Abbas mov'd,

" And every Georgian maid like Abra lov'd!"

Yet, 'midst the blaze of courts she fix'd her love

On the cool fountain, or the shady grove;

Still with the shepherd's innocence her mind

To the sweet vale, and flowery mead inclin'd;

And oft as Spring renewed the plains with flowers,

Breath'd his soft gales, and led the fragrant hours,

With sure return she sought the sylvan scene,

The breezy mountains, and the forests green.

Her maids around her mov'd, a duteous band!

Each bore a crook all rural in her hand:

Some simple lay, of flocks and herds they sung;

With joy the mountain and the forest rung.

" Be every youth like royal Abbas mov'd,

" And every Georgian maid like Abra lov'd!"

And oft the royal lover left the care

And thorns of state, attendant on the fair;

Oft to the shades and low-roof'd cots retir'd,

Or sought the vale where first his heart was fir'd:

A russet mantle, like a swain, he wore,

And thought of crowns and busy courts no more.

    " Be every youth like royal Abbas mov'd,

    " And every Georgian maid like Abra lov'd!"

Blest was the life that royal Abbas led:

Sweet was his love, and innocent his bed.

What if in wealth the noble maid excel;

The simple shepherd girl can love as well.

Let those who rule on Persia's jewel'd throne,

Be fam'd for love, and gentlest love alone;

Or wreath, like Abbas, full of fair renown,

The lover's myrtle with the warrior's crown.

O happy days! the maids around her say;

O haste, profuse of blessings, haste away!

" Be every youth, like royal Abbas mov'd;

" And every Georgian maid like Abra lov'd!"

ECLOGUE IV.

AGIB AND SECANDER; OR, THE FUGITIVES.

SCENE, A MOUNTAIN IN CIRCASSIA.

TIME, MIDNIGHT.

IN fair Circassia, where, to love inclin'd,

Each swain was blest, for every maid was kind;

At that still hour, when awful midnight reigns,

And none but wretches haunt the twilight plains;

What time the Moon had hung her lamp on high,

And past in radiance thro' the cloudless sky;

Sad o'er the dews two brother shepherds fled,

Where wildering fear and desperate sorrow led:

Fast as they prest their flight, behind them lay

Wild ravag'd plains, and vallies stole away.

Along the mountain's bending sides they ran,

Till faint and weak Secander thus began:

SECANDER.

Oh, stay thee, Agib, for my feet deny,

No longer friendly to my life, to flie.

Friend of my heart! Oh turn thee and survey,

Trace our long flight through all its length of way!

And first review that long-extended plain,

And yon wide groves, already past with pain!

Yon ragged cliff, whose dangerous path we tried!

And last, this lofty mountain's weary side!

AGIB.

Weak as thou art, yet hapless must thou know

The toils of flight, or some severer woe!

Still as I haste, the Tartar shouts behind,

And shrieks and sorrows load the saddening wind:

In rage of heart, with ruin in his hand,

He blasts our harvests, and deforms our land.

Yon citron grove, whence first in fear we came,

Droops its fair honours to the conquering flame:

Far fly the swains, like us, in deep despair,

And leave to ruffian bands their fleecy care.

SECANDER.

Unhappy land! whose blessings tempt the sword,

In vain, unheard, thou call'st thy Persian lord!

In vain thou court'st him, helpless, to thine aid,

To shield the shepherd, and protect the maid!

Far off, in thoughtless indolence resign'd,

Soft dreams of love and pleasure sooth his mind;

'Midst fair sultanas lost in idle joy,

No wars alarm him, and no fears annoy.

AGIB.

Yet these green hills, in summer's sultry heat,

Have lent the monarch oft a cool retreat.

Sweet to the sight is Zabran's flowery plain,

And once by maids and shepherds lov'd in vain!

No more the virgins shall delight to rove

By Sargis' banks, or Irwan's shady grove;

On Tarkie's mountains catch the cooling gale,

Or breathe the sweets of Aly's flowery vale:

Fair scenes! but, ah! no more with peace possest,

With ease alluring, and with plenty blest!

No more the shepherds' whitening tents appear,

Nor the kind products of a bounteous year;

No more the date, with snowy blossoms crown'd!

But Ruin spreads her baleful fires around.

SECANDER.

In vain Circassia boasts her spicy groves,

For **ever** fam'd for pure and happy loves:

In vain she boasts her fairest of the fair,

Their eyes' blue languish, and their golden hair.

Those eyes in tears their fruitless grief must send;

Those hairs the Tartar's cruel hand shall rend.

AGIB.

Ye Georgian swains, that piteous learn from far —

Circassia's ruin, and the waste of war:

Some weightier arms than crooks and staffs prepare,

To shield your harvests, and defend your fair:

The Turk and Tartar like designs pursue,

Fix'd to destroy, and steadfast to undo.

Wild as his land, in native deserts bred,

By lust incited, or by malice led,

The villain Arab, as he prowls for prey,

Oft marks with blood and wasting flames the way;

Yet none so cruel as the Tartar foe,

To death inur'd, and nurst in scenes of woe.

He said: when loud along the vale was heard

A shriller shriek, and nearer fires appear'd.

Th' affrighted shepherds thro' the dews of night,

Wide o'er the moon-light hills renew'd their flight.

ODES,

DESCRIPTIVE AND ALLEGORICAL.

1746

ODE TO PITY.

O THOU! the friend of man assign'd,

With balmy hands his wounds to bind,

   And charm his frantic woe:

When first Distress, with dagger keen,

Broke forth to waste his destin'd scene,

   His wild unsated foe!

By Pella's bard, a magic name,

By all the griefs his thought could frame,

   Receive my humble rite:

Long, Pity, let the nations view

Thy sky-worn robes of tenderest blue,

   And eyes of dewy light!

But wherefore need I wander wide

To old Ilissus' distant side,

    Deserted stream and mute?

Wild Arun* too has heard thy strains,

And Echo, 'midst my native plains,

    Been sooth'd by Pity's lute.

There first the wren thy myrtles shed

On gentlest Otway's infant head,

    To him thy cell was shown;

And while he sung the female heart,

With youth's soft notes unspoil'd by art,

    Thy turtles mix'd their own.

      * A river in Sussex.

Come, Pity! come; by Fancy's aid,

Ev'n now my thoughts, relenting maid,

    Thy temple's pride design:

Its southern site, its truth complete,

Shall raise a wild enthusiast heat

    In all who view the shrine.

There Picture's toil shall well relate,

How chance, or hard involving fate,

    O'er mortal bliss prevail:

The buskin'd Muse shall near her stand,

And sighing prompt her tender hand,

    With each disastrous tale.

There let me oft, retir'd by day,

In dreams of passion melt away.

Allow'd with thee to dwell:

There waste the mournful lamp of night,

'Till, Virgin, thou again delight

    To hear a British shell!

Thou, to whom the world unknown

With all its shadowy shapes is shown;

Who seest appall'd th' unreal scene,

While Fancy lifts the veil between:

    Ah Fear! ah, frantic Fear!

    I see, I see thee near.

I know thy hurried step, thy haggard eye!

Like thee I start, like thee disorder'd fly,

    For, lo! what monsters in thy train appear!

Danger, whose limbs of giant mold

What mortal eye can fix'd behold?

Who stalks his round, an hideous form,

Howling amidst the midnight storm;

Or throws him on the ridgy steep

Of some loose hanging rock to sleep:

And with him thousand phantoms join'd,

Who prompt to deeds accurs'd the mind :

And those, the fiends, who near allied,

O'er Nature's wounds, and wrecks preside ;

While Vengeance, in the lurid air,

Lifts her red arm, expos'd and bare :

On whom that ravening brood of Fate,

Who lap the blood of Sorrow, wait ;

Who, Fear, this ghastly train can see,

And look not madly wild, like thee ?

EPODE.

In earliest Greece, to thee, with partial choice,

   The grief-full Muse addrest her infant tongue

The maids and matrons, on her awful voice,

Silent and pale, in wild amazement hung.

Yet he, the Bard* who first invok'd thy name,

  Disdain'd in Marathon its power to feel:

For not alone he nurs'd the poet's flame,

  But reach'd from Virtue's hand the patriot's steel.

But who is he, whom later garlands grace,

  Who left awhile o'er Hybla's dews to rove,

With trembling eyes thy dreary steps to trace,

  Where thou and furies shar'd the baleful grove?

Wrapt in thy cloudy veil th' incestuous Queen †

  Sigh'd the sad call her son and husband heard,

When once alone it broke the silent scene,

  And he the wretch of Thebes no more appear'd.

* Æfchylus. † Jocafta.

O Fear ! I know thee by my throbbing heart,

   Thy withering power inspir'd each mournful line

Tho' gentle Pity claim her mingled part,

   Yet all the thunders of the scenes are thine !

ANTISTROPHE.

Thou who such weary lengths hast past,

Where wilt thou rest, mad Nymph ! at last ?

Say, wilt thou shroud in haunted cell,

Where gloomy Rape and Murder dwell ?

   Or in some hallow'd seat,

   'Gainst which the big waves beat,

Hear drowning seamens' cries in tempests brought !

Dark Power ! with shuddering, meek, submitted

  thought,

Be mine to read the visions old,

Which thy awakening bards have told.

T. Stothard del. R.A.   J. Heath R.A. Sculp.

Or in some hallow'd Seat,

'Gainst which the big Waves beat,

Hear drowning Seamen's Cries in Tempests brought.

Published by Cadell & Davies, Strand, Sep.r 1.st 1797.

And, lest thou meet my blasted view,

'Hold each strange tale devoutly true;

Ne'er be I found, by thee o'er-aw'd,

In that thrice-hallow'd eve abroad,

When ghosts, as cottage-maids believe,

Their pebbled beds permitted leave,

And goblins haunt from fire, or fen,

Or mine, or flood, the walks of men!

O thou, whose spirit most possest

The sacred seat of Shakspeare's **breast** !

By all that from thy prophet broke,

In thy divine emotions spoke !

Hither again thy fury **deal,**

Teach me **but** once like him to feel :

His cypress wreath my meed decree,

And I, O Fear, will dwell with thee !

ODE TO SIMPLICITY. √

O THOU by Nature taught,

To breathe her genuine thought,

In numbers warmly pure, and sweetly strong:

Who first on mountains wild,

In Fancy, loveliest child,

Thy babe, and Pleasure's, nurs'd the powers of so

Thou, who with hermit heart

Disdain'st the wealth of art,

And gauds, and pageant weeds, and trailing pall:

But com'st a decent maid,

In Attic robe array'd,

O chaste, unboastful nymph! to thee I call!

By all the honey'd store

On Hybla's thymy shore,

By all her blooms, and mingled murmurs dear,

By her, whose love-lorn woe,

In evening musings slow,

Sooth'd sweetly sad Electra's poet's ear:

By old Cephisus' deep,

Who spread his wavy sweep

In warbled wanderings round thy green retreat,

On whose enamell'd side;

When holy Freedom died,

No equal haunt allur'd thy future feet.

O sister meek of Truth,

To my admiring youth

Thy sober aid and native charms infuse!

The flowers that sweetest breathe,

Tho' beauty cull'd the wreath,

Still ask thy hand to range their order'd hues.

While Rome could none esteem

But virtue's patriot theme,

You lov'd her hills, and led her laureate band;

But staid to sing alone

To one distinguish'd throne,

And turn'd thy face, and fled her alter'd land.

No more, in hall or bower,

The passions own thy power,

Love, only love, her forceless numbers mean :

For thou hast left her shrine,

Nor olive more, nor vine,

Shall gain thy feet to bless the servile scene.

Tho' taste, tho' genius, bless

To some divine excess,

Faint's the cold work till thou inspire the whole

What each, what all supply,

May court, may charm our eye,

Thou ! only thou can'st raise the meeting soul !

Of these let others ask,

To aid some mighty task,

I only seek to find thy temperate vale :

Where oft my reed might sound,

To maids and shepherds round.

And all thy sons, O Nature ! learn my tale.

ODE ON THE POETICAL CHARACTER.

As once, if not with light regard,

I read aright that gifted Bard,

(Him whose school above the rest

His loveliest Elfin queen has blest)

One, only one, unrivall'd fair *,

Might hope the magic girdle wear,

At solemn turney hung on high,

The wish of each love-darting eye.

Lo ! to each other nymph in turn applied,

　As if, in air unseen, some hovering hand,

Some chaste and angel-friend to virgin-fame,

　With whisper'd spell had burst the starting band,

---

* Florimel. See Spenfer, Leg. 4th.

It left unblest her loath'd dishonour'd side;

    Happier hopeless fair, if never

    Her baffled hand with vain endeavour

Had touch'd that fatal zone to her denied!

Young Fancy thus, to me divinest name,

    To whom, prepar'd and bath'd in heaven,

    The cest of amplest power is given,

    To few the god-like gift assigns,

    To gird their blest prophetic loins.

And gaze her visions wild, and feel unmix'd her flame.

    The band as fairy legends say,

    Was wove on that creating day,

    When He, who call'd with thought to birth

    Yon tented sky, this laughing earth,

    And drest with springs, and forests tall,

    And pour'd the main engirting all,

Long by the lov'd Enthusiast wooed

Himself in some diviner mood,

Retiring, sat with her alone,

And plac'd her on his sapphire throne,

The whiles, the vaulted shrine around,

Seraphic wires were heard to sound,

Now sublimest triumph swelling;

Now on love and mercy dwelling;

And she, from out the veiling cloud,

Breath'd her magic notes aloud:

And thou, thou rich-hair'd youth of morn,

And all thy subject life was born!

The dangerous passions kept aloof,

Far from the sainted growing woof:

But near it sat ecstatic Wonder,

Listening the deep applauding thunder:

And Truth, in sunny vest array'd,

By whose the Tarsel's eyes were made;

And the shadowy tribes of Mind,

In braided dance their murmurs join'd,

And all the bright uncounted Powers,

Who feed on heaven's ambrosial flowers.

Where is the Bard, whose soul can now

Its high presuming hopes avow ?

Where he who thinks, with rapture blind,

This hallow'd work for him design'd ?

High on some cliff, to heaven up-pil'd,

Of rude access, of prospect wild,

Where, tangled round the jealous steep,

Strange shades o'erbrow the vallies deep,

And holy Genii guard the rock,

Its glooms embrown, its springs unlock,

While on its rich ambitious head,

An Eden, like his own, lies spread,

I view that oak, the fancied glades among,

By which, as Milton lay, his evening ear,

From many a cloud that dropp'd ethereal dew,

Night spher'd in heaven its native strains could hear :

On which that ancient trump he reach'd was hung ;

Thither oft his glory greeting,

From Waller's myrtle shades retreating,

With many a vow from Hope's aspiring tongue,

My trembling feet his guiding steps pursue ;

In vain—Such bliss to one alone,

Of all the sons of soul was known,

And Heaven, and Fancy, kindred powers,

Have now o'erturned th' inspiring bowers,

Or curtain'd close such scene from every future view.

O D E,

WRITTEN IN THE YEAR M DCC XLVI.

HOW sleep the brave, who sink to rest,

By all their country's wishes blest!

When Spring, with dewy fingers cold,

Returns to deck their hallow'd mold,

She there shall dress a sweeter sod,

Than Fancy's feet have ever trod.

By Fairy hands their knell is rung,

By forms unseen their dirge is sung:

There Honour comes, a pilgrim grey,

To bless the turf that wraps their clay,

And Freedom shall awhile repair,

To dwell a weeping hermit there!

Drawn by T. Stothard *R.A.*　　　　　　Engᵈ by I. Parker.

Oft with thy Bosom bare art found,
Pleading for him the Youth who sinks to Ground:

Published by Cadell & Davies, Strand, Sepᵗ 1ˢᵗ 1797.

ODE TO MERCY.

O THOU! who sit'st a smiling bride

By Valour's arm'd and awful side,

Gentlest of sky-born forms, and best ador'd:

Who oft, with songs, divine to hear,

Win'st from his fatal grasp the spear,

And hid'st in wreaths of flowers his bloodless sword!

Thou who, amidst the deathful field,

By godlike chiefs alone beheld,

Oft with thy bosom bare art found,

Pleading for him, the youth who sinks to ground:

See, Mercy, see! with pure and loaded hands,

Before thy shrine my country's Genius stands,

And decks thy altar still, tho' pierc'd with many a

wound!

F.

ANTISTROPHE.

When he whom even our **joys** provoke,

The Fiend **of** Nature join'd his **yoke,**

And rush'd in wrath to make our isle his prey;

Thy form, from out thy sweet abode,

O'ertook him on his blasted road,

And stopp'd his wheels, and look'd his rage away.

I see recoil his sable steeds,

That bore him swift to savage deeds,

Thy tender melting eyes they own;

O Maid! for all thy love to Britain shown,

Where Justice bars her iron tower,

To thee we build a roseate bower,

Thou, thou, shalt rule our queen, and share our

monarch's throne!

ODE TO LIBERTY.

WHO shall awake the Spartan fife,

And call in solemn sounds to life

The youths, whose locks divinely spreading,

Like vernal hyacinths in sullen hue,

At once the breath of fear and virtue shedding,

Applauding Freedom lov'd of old to view?

What new Alcæus, fancy-blest,

Shall sing the sword, in myrtles drest,

At Wisdom's shrine awhile its flame concealing,

(What place so fit to seal a deed renown'd?)

Till she her brightest lightnings round revealing,

It leap'd in glory forth, and dealt her prompted

wound!

O Goddess! in that feeling hour,

When most its sounds would court thy ears,

    Let not my shell's misguided power

E'er draw thy sad, thy mindful tears.

    No, Freedom! no, I will not tell,

How Rome, before thy weeping face,

    With heaviest sound, a giant statue, fell,

Push'd by a wild and artless race,

From off its wide ambitious base,

When Time his northern sons of spoil awoke,

    And all the blended work of strength and grace,

With many a rude repeated stroke,

And many a barbarous yell, to thousand fragments

    broke!

EPODE 1.

Yet even, where'er the least appear'd,

Th' admiring world thy hand rever'd:

Still, 'midst the scatter'd states around,

Some remnants of her strength were found;

They saw, by what escap'd the storm,

How wondrous rose her perfect form,

How in the great, the labour'd whole,

Each mighty master pour'd his soul;

For sunny Florence, seat of art,

Beneath her vines preserv'd a part.

Till they, whom Science lov'd to name,

(Oh! who could fear it?) quench'd her flame.

And lo, an humbler relic laid

In jealous Pisa's olive shade!

See small Marino joins the theme,

Tho' least, not last in thy esteem;

Strike, louder strike th' ennobling strings

To those, whose merchant-sons were kings;

To him, who deck'd with pearly pride,

In Adria weds his green-hair'd bride:

Hail, port of glory, wealth, and pleasure!

Ne'er let me change this Lydian measure:

Nor e'er her former pride relate,

To sad Liguria's bleeding state.

Ah, no! more pleas'd thy haunts I seek,

On wild Helvetia's mountains bleak:

(Where, when the favour'd of thy choice,

The daring archer heard thy voice;

Forth from his eyrie rous'd in dread,

The ravening eagle northward fled.)

Or dwell in willow'd meads more near,

With those* to whom thy Stork is dear:

* The Dutch, amongst whom there are very severe penalties
for those who are convicted of killing this bird. They are
kept tame in almost all their towns, and particularly at the
Hague; of the arms of which they make a part. The common

Those whom the rod of Alva bruis'd,

Whose crown a British queen refus'd,

The magic works, thou feel'st the strains,

One holier name alone remains;

The perfect spell shall then avail,

Hail Nymph! ador'd by Britain, hail!

ANTISTROPHE.

Beyond the measure vast of thought,

The works, the wizard Time has wrought!

The Gaul, 'tis held of antique story,

Saw Britain link'd to his now adverse strand,*

No sea between, nor cliff sublime and hoary,

He pass'd with unwet feet thro' all our land.

people of Holland are said to entertain a superstitious sentiment, that if the whole species of them should become extinct,
they should lose their liberties.

* This tradition is mentioned by several of **our** old histori-
ans. Some naturalists too have endeavoured to support the
probability of the fact, by arguments drawn from the correspondent disposition of the two opposite coasts.

To the blown Baltic then, they say,

The wild waves found another way,

Where Orcas howls, his wolfish mountains rounding,

Till all the banded west at once 'gan rise,

A wide wild storm even Nature's self confounding,

Withering her giant sons with strange uncouth

surprise.

This pillar'd earth, so firm and wide,

By winds and inward labours torn,

In thunders dread was push'd aside,

And down the shouldering billows borne.

And see like gems, her laughing train,

The little isles on every side;

Mona*, once hid from those who search the main,

Where thousand Elfin shapes abide,

---

* There is a tradition in the Isle of Man, that a mermaid be-
coming enamoured of a young man of extraordinary beauty,
took an opportunity of meeting him one day as he walked on

And Wight who checks the westering tide,

  For thee consenting Heaven has each bestow'd,

A fair attendant on her sovereign pride:

  To thee this blest divorce she ow'd,

For thou hast made her vales thy lov'd, thy last

    abode!

SECOND EPODE.

Then, too, 'tis said, an hoary pile,

'Midst the green navel of our isle,

Thy shrine in some religious wood,

O soul-enforcing Goddess! stood;

There oft the painted native's feet

Were wont thy form celestial meet :

the shore, and opened her passion to him, but was received
with a coldness, occasioned by his horror and surprise at
her appearance. This, however, was so misconstrued by the
sea-lady, **that** in revenge for his treatment of her, she punished
the whole island with a mist, so that all who attempted to carry
on any commerce with it, either never arrived at it, but wan-
dered up and down the sea, or were upon a sudden wrecked
upon its cliffs.

Tho' now with hopeless toil we trace

Time's backward rolls, to find its place;

Whether the fiery-tressèd Dane,

Or Roman's self, o'erturn'd the fane;

Or in what heaven-left age it fell;

'Twere hard for modern song to tell.

Yet still, if Truth those beams infuse,

Which guide at once, and charm the Muse,

Beyond yon braided clouds that lie,

Paving the light-embroider'd sky:

Amidst the bright pavilion'd plains,

The beauteous model still remains.

There happier than in islands blest,

Or bowers by Spring or Hebe drest,

The chiefs who fill our Albion's story,

In warlike weeds, retir'd in glory,

Hear their consorted Druids sing
Their triumphs to th' immortal string.

How may the poet now unfold,
What never tongue or numbers told?
How learn, delighted and amaz'd,
What hands unknown that fabric rais'd?
Ev'n now, before his favour'd eyes,
In Gothic pride it seems to rise!
Yet Grecia's graceful orders join,
Majestic thro' the mix'd design:
The secret builder knew to choose
Each sphere-found gem of richest hues:
Whate'er heaven's purer mold contains,
When nearer suns emblaze its veins:

There on the walls the Patriot's sight

May ever hang with fresh delight,

And, grav'd with some prophetic rage,

Read Albion's fame thro' every age.

Ye forms divine ! ye laureate band

That near her inmost altar stand,

Now sooth her to her blissful train,

Blithe Concord's social form to gain:

Concord, whose myrtle wand can steep

Even Anger's blood-shot eyes in sleep !

Before whose breathing bosom's balm,

Rage drops his steel, and storms grow calm;

Here let our sires and matrons hoar

Welcome to Britain's ravag'd shore,

Our youths, enamour'd of the fair,

Play with the tangles of her hair,

Till, in one loud applauding sound,

The nations shout to her around,

Oh how supremely art thou blest?

Thou, Lady, thou shalt rule the West!

ODE

TO A LADY,

ON THE DEATH OF COLONEL CHARLES ROSS,

IN THE ACTION AT FONTENOY.

WRITTEN MAY, M DCC XLV.

WHILE, lost to all his former mirth,

Britannia's genius bends to earth,

    And mourns the fatal day:

While stain'd with blood he strives to tear,

Unseemly, from his sea-green hair,

    The wreaths of cheerful May:

The thoughts which musing Pity pays,

And fond Remembrance loves to raise,

Your faithful hours attend:

Still Fancy, to herself unkind,

Awakes to grief the soften'd mind,

    And points the bleeding friend.

By rapid Scheldt's descending wave,

His country's vows shall bless the grave,

    Where'er the youth is laid :

That sacred spot the village hind

With every sweetest turf shall bind,

    And Peace protect the shade.

O'er him, whose doom thy virtues grieve,

Aërial forms shall sit at eve,

And bend the pensive head!

And, fallen to save his injur'd land,

Imperial Honour's awful hand

    Shall point his lonely bed!

The warlike dead of every age,

Who fill the fair recording page,

    Shall leave their sainted rest:

And, half-reclining on his spear,

Each wondring chief by turns appear,

    To hail the blooming guest.

Old Edward's sons, unknown to yield,

Shall crowd from Cressy's laurell'd field,

And gaze with fix'd delight :

Again for Britain's wrongs they feel,

Again they snatch the gleamy steel,

   And wish th' avenging fight.

But lo, where, sunk in deep despair,

Her garments torn, her bosom bare,

   Impatient Freedom lies !

Her matted tresses madly spread,

To every sod which wraps the dead,

   She turns her joyless eyes.

Ne'er shall she leave that lowly ground,

Till notes of triumph bursting round,

F

Proclaim her reign restor'd :

Till William seek the sad retreat,

And bleeding at her sacred feet,

    Present the sated sword.

If, weak to sooth so soft an heart,

These pictur'd glories nought impart,

    To dry thy constant tear :

If yet, in Sorrow's distant eye,

Expos'd and pale thou seest him lie,

    Wild war insulting near:

Where'er from time thou court'st relief,

The Muse shall still, with social grief,

Her gentlest promise keep:

Even humble Harting's cottag'd vale,

Shall learn the sad repeated tale,

  And bid her shepherds weep.

ODE TO EVENING.

IF aught of oaten stop, or pastoral song,

  May hope, chaste Eve, to sooth thy modest ear,

      Like thy own solemn springs,

      Thy springs, and dying gales,

  O Nymph reserv'd ! while now the bright-hair'd sun

  Sits in yon western tent, whose cloudy skirts,

      With brede ethereal wove,

      O'erhang his wavy bed:

Now air is hush'd, save where the weak-ey'd bat,

With short shrill shriek flits by on leathern wing,

    Or where the beetle winds

    His small but sullen horn?

As oft he rises 'midst the twilight path,

Against the pilgrim borne in heedless hum :

    Now teach me, Maid compos'd,

    To breathe some soften'd strain,

Whose numbers stealing thro' thy dark'ning vale,

May not unseemly with its stillness suit,

    As musing slow, I hail

    Thy genial lov'd return !

For when thy folding-star arising shows

His paly circlet, at his warning lamp

    The fragrant Hours, and Elves

    Who slept in buds the day,

And many a Nymph who wreathes her brows with sed

And sheds the freshening dew, and lovelier still,

    The pensive Pleasures sweet

    Prepare thy shadowy car.

Then let me rove some wild and heathy scene,

Or find some ruin 'midst its dreary dells,

    Whose walls more awful nod

    By thy religious gleams.

Or if chill blust'ring winds, or driving rain,

Prevent my willing feet, be mine the hut,

That from the mountain's side,

Views wilds and swelling floods,

And hamlets brown, and dim-discover'd spires,

And hears their simple bell, and marks o'er all

Thy dewy fingers draw

The gradual dusky veil.

While Spring shall pour his showers, as oft he wont,

And bathe thy breathing tresses, meekest Eve!

While Summer loves to sport

Beneath thy lingering light?

While sallow Autumn fills thy lap with leaves,

Or Winter, yellow thro' the troublous air,

    Affrights thy shrinking train,

    And rudely rends thy robes:

So long regardful of thy quiet rule,

Shall Fancy, Friendship, Science, smiling Peace,

    Thy gentlest influence own,

    And love thy favourite name!

ODE TO PEACE.

O THOU! who bad'st thy turtles bear

Swift from his grasp thy golden hair,

    And sought'st thy native skies:

When War, by vultures drawn from far,

To Britain bent his iron car,

    And bade his storms arise!

Tir'd of his rude tyrannic sway,

Our youth shall fix some festive day,

    His sullen shrines to burn:

But thou, who hear'st the turning spheres,

What sounds may charm thy partial ears,

    And gain thy blest return!

O Peace ! thy injur'd robes up-bind !

Oh rise, and leave not one behind

    Of all thy beamy train :

The British lion, Goddess sweet !

Lies stretch'd on earth to kiss thy feet,

    And own thy holier reign.

Let others court thy transient smile,

But come to grace thy western isle,

    By warlike Honor led !

And, while around her ports rejoice,

While all her sons adore thy choice,

    With him for ever wed !.

THE MANNERS.

AN ODE.

FAREWELL, for clearer ken design'd;

The dim-discover'd tracts of mind:

Truths which, from action's paths retir'd,

My silent search in vain requir'd,

No more my sail that deep explores,

No more I search those magic shores,

What regions part the world of soul,

Or whence thy streams, Opinion, roll:

If e'er I round such Fairy field,

Some power impart the spear and shield,

At which the wizard Passions fly,

By which the giant Follies die!

Farewell the porch, whose roof is seen,

Arch'd with th' enlivening olive's green :

Where Science, prank'd in tissued **vest,**

By Reason, Pride, and Fancy drest,

Comes like a bride, so trim array'd,

To wed with Doubt in Plato's shade !

Youth of the quick uncheated sight,

Thy walks, Observance, more invite !

O thou, who lov'st that ampler range,

Where life's wide prospects round thee change,

And, with her mingled sons allied,

Throw'st the prattling page aside ;

To me in converse sweet impart,

To read in man the native heart,

To learn, where Science sure is found,

From Nature as she lives around;

And gazing oft her mirror true,

By turns each shifting image view!

Till meddling Art's officious lore,

Reverse the lessons taught before,

Alluring from a safer rule,

To dream in her enchanted school;

Thou, Heaven, whate'er of great we boast,

Hast blest this social science most.

Retiring hence to thoughtful cell,

As Fancy breathes her potent spell,

Not vain she finds the charmful task,

In pageant quaint, in motley mask,

Behold, before her musing eyes,

The countless Manners round her rise;

While ever varying as they pass,

To some Contempt applies her glass:

With these the white-rob'd Maids combine,

And those the laughing Satyrs join!

But who is he whom now she views,

In robe of wild contending hues?

Thou by the passions nurs'd; I greet

The comic sock that binds thy feet!

O Humour, thou whose name is known

To Britain's favour'd isle alone:

Me too amidst thy band admit,

There where the young-eyed healthful Wit,

(Whose jewels in his crisped hair

Are plac'd each other's beams to share,

Whom no delights from thee divide)

In laughter loos'd attends thy side!

By old Miletus * who so long

Has ceas'd his love-inwoven song :

By all you taught the Tuscan maids,

In chang'd Italia's modern shades :

By him †, whose Knight's distinguish'd name,

Refin'd a nation's lust of fame ;

Whose tales even now, with echos sweet,

Castilia's Moorish hills repeat :

Or him ‡, whom Seine's blue nymphs deplore,

In watchet weeds on Gallia's shore.

* Alluding to the Milesian Tales, some of the earliest
romances.

† Cervantes.

‡ Monsieur Le Sage, author of the incomparable adventures
of Gil Blas de Santillane, who died in Paris in the year 1745.

Who drew the sad Sicilian maid,

By virtues in her sire betray'd:

   O Nature boon, from whom proceed

Each forceful thought, each prompted deed;

If but from thee I hope to feel,

On all my heart imprint thy seal!

Let some retreating Cynic find

Those oft-turn'd scrolls I leave behind,

The Sports and I this hour agree,

To rove thy scene-ful world with thee!

THE PASSIONS. VI.

AN ODE FOR MUSIC.

WHEN Music, heavenly maid, was young,

While yet in early Greece she sung,

The Passions oft, to hear her shell,

Throng'd around her magic cell,

Exulting, trembling, raging, fainting,

Possest beyond the Muse's painting;

By turns they felt the glowing mind

Disturb'd, delighted, rais'd, refin'd.

'Till once, 'tis said, when all were fir'd,

Fill'd with fury, rapt, inspir'd,

From the supporting myrtles round

They snatch'd her instruments of sound,

And, as they oft had heard apart

Sweet lessons of her forceful art,

Each, for Madness rul'd the hour,

Would prove his own expressive power.

First Fear, his hand its skill to try,

Amid the chords bewilder'd laid,

And back recoil'd, he knew not why,

Even at the sound himself had made.

Next Anger rush'd, his eyes on fire,

In lightnings own'd his secret stings,

In one rude clash he struck the lyre,

And swept with hurried hand the strings.

With woful measures wan Despair—

    Low sullen sounds his grief beguil'd,

A sullen, strange, and mingled air,

    'Twas sad by fits, by starts 'twas wild.

But thou, O Hope! with eyes so fair,

    What was thy delighted measure?

    Still it whisper'd promis'd pleasure,

And bade the lovely scenes at distance hail!

    Still would her touch the strain prolong,

And from the rocks, the woods, the vale,

    She call'd on Echo still thro' all the song;

    And where her sweetest theme she chose,

    A soft responsive voice was heard at every close,

And Hope enchanted smil'd, and wav'd her golden

    hair.

And longer had she sung,—but, with a frown,

    Revenge impatient rose,

He threw his blood-stain'd sword in thunder down,

    And, with a withering look,

    The war-denouncing trumpet took,

And blew a blast so loud and dread,

Were ne'er prophetic sounds so full of woe.

    And ever and anon he beat

    The doubling drum with furious heat;

   And tho' sometimes, each dreary pause between

    Dejected Pity at his side,

    Her soul-subduing voice applied,

Yet still he kept his wild unalter'd mien,

While each strain'd ball of sight seem'd bursting

    from his head.

T. Stothard R.A. del.   J. Heath R.A. Sculp.

They saw in Tempe's Vale her native Maids,

Amidst the festal sounding Shades,

To some unwearied Minstrel dancing.

Published by Cadell & Davies, Strand, Sep.ʳ 1.ᵗ 1797

Thy numbers, Jealousy, to nought were fix'd,

    Sad **proof** of thy distressful state,

Of differing themes the veering song was mix'd,

    And now it courted Love, now raving call'd on

        Hate.

    With eyes up-rais'd, as one inspir'd,

    Pale Melancholy sat retir'd,

    And from her wild sequester'd seat,

    In notes by distance made more sweet,

Pour'd thro' the mellow horn her pensive soul:

    And dashing soft from rocks around,

    Bubbling runnels join'd the sound ;

Thro' glades and glooms the mingled measure stole,

Or o'er some haunted streams with fond delay,

    Round an holy calm diffusing,

    Love of peace and lonely musing,

In hollow murmurs died away.

    But Oh, how alter'd was its sprightlier tone!

When Cheerfulness, a nymph of healthiest hue,

    Her bow across her shoulders flung,

Her buskins gemm'd with morning dew,

    Blew an inspiring air that dale and thicket rung,

        The hunter's call to Faun and Dryad known;

The oak-crown'd Sisters, and their chaste-eyed quee:

Satyrs and Sylvan boys were seen,

Peeping from forth their alleys green;

Brown Exercise rejoic'd to hear,

And Sport leapt up, and seiz'd his beechen spear.

Last came Joy's ecstatic trial ;

   He with viny crown advancing,

  First to the lively pipe his hand addrest,

But soon he saw the brisk awakening viol,

   Whose sweet entrancing voice he lov'd the best.

    They would have thought who heard the strain,

    They saw in Tempe's vale her native maids,

    Amidst the festal sounding shades,

    To some unwearied minstrel dancing,

  While, as his flying fingers kiss'd the strings,

    Love fram'd with Mirth, a gay fantastic round,

    Loose were her tresses seen, her zone unbound,

    And he, amidst his frolic play,

    As if he would the charming air repay,

  Shook thousand odours from his dewy wings.

O Music, sphere-descended maid,

Friend of pleasure, wisdom's aid,

Why, Goddess, why to us denied,

Lay'st thou thy ancient lyre aside?

As in that lov'd Athenian bower,

You learn'd an all-commanding power,

Thy mimic soul, O nymph endear'd!

Can well recall what then it heard.

Where is thy native simple heart,

Devote to virtue, fancy, art?

Arise, as in that elder time,

Warm, energetic, chaste, sublime!

Thy wonders, in that god-like age,

Fill thy recording Sister's page—

'Tis said, and I believe the tale,

Thy humblest reed could more prevail,

Had more of strength, diviner rage,

Than all which charms this laggard age,

Even all at once together found

Cecilia's mingled world of sound—

O bid our vain endeavours cease,

Revive the just designs of Greece,

Return in all thy simple state!

Confirm the tales her sons relate!

AN EPISTLE,

ADDRESSED TO SIR THOMAS HANMER,

ON HIS

EDITION OF SHAKSPEARE'S WORKS.

WHILE born to bring the Muse's happier days,

A patriot's hand protects a poet's lays,

While nurs'd by you she sees her myrtles bloom,

Green and unwither'd o'er his honour'd tomb:

Excuse her doubts, if yet she fears to tell

What secret transports in her bosom swell:

With conscious awe she hears the critic's fame,

And blushing hides her wreath at Shakspeare's name.

Hard was the lot those injur'd strains endur'd,

Unown'd by Science, and by years obscur'd:

Fair Fancy wept; and echoing sighs confess'd

A fixt despair in every tuneful breast.

Not with more grief th' afflicted swains appear,

When wintry winds deform the plenteous year;

When lingering frosts the ruin'd seats invade,

Where Peace resorted, and the Graces play'd.

Each rising art by just gradation moves,

Toil builds on toil, and age on age improves:

The Muse alone unequal dealt her rage,

And grac'd with noblest pomp her earliest stage.

Preserv'd thro' time, the speaking scenes impart

Each changeful wish of Phædra's tortur'd heart:

Or paint the curse that mark'd the * Theban's reign,

A bed incestuous, and a father slain.

* The Œdipus of Sophocles.

With kind concern our pitying eyes o'erflow,

Trace the sad tale, and own another's woe.

To Rome remov'd, with wit secure to please,

The comic sisters kept their native ease.

With jealous fear declining Greece beheld

Her own Menander's art almost excell'd!

But every Muse essay'd to raise in vain

Some labour'd rival of her tragic strain;

Ilyssus' laurels, tho' transferr'd with toil,

Droop'd their fair leaves, nor knew th' unfriendly soi.

As arts expir'd resistless Dullness rose;

Goths, priests, or Vandals,—all were learning's foes.

Till * Julius first recall'd each exil'd maid,

And Cosmo own'd them in th' Etrurian shade:

* Julius II. the immediate predecessor of Leo X.

Then deeply skill'd in love's engaging theme,

The soft Provençal pass'd to Arno's stream :

With graceful ease the wanton lyre he strung,

Sweet flow'd the lays—but love was all he sung.

The gay description could not fail to move;

For, led by nature, all are friends to love.

But Heaven, still various in its works, decreed

The perfect boast of time should last succeed.

The beauteous union must appear at length,

Of Tuscan fancy, and Athenian strength :

One greater Muse Eliza's reign adorn,

And even a Shakspeare to her fame be born!

Yet, ah ! so bright her morning's opening ray,

In vain our Britain hop'd an equal day!

No second growth the western isle could bear,

At once exhausted with too rich a year.

Too nicely Jonson knew the critic's part;

Nature in him was almost lost in art.

Of softer mold the gentle Fletcher came,

The next in order, as the next in name.

With pleas'd attention 'midst his scenes we find

Each glowing thought that warms the female mind;

Each melting sigh, and every tender tear,

The lover's wishes, and the virgin's fear.

His * every strain the Smiles and Graces own;

But stronger Shakspeare felt for man alone:

Drawn by his pen, our ruder passions stand

Th' unrivall'd picture of his early hand.

* Their characters are thus distinguished by Mr. Dryden.

* With gradual steps, and slow, exacter France

Saw Art's fair empire o'er her shores advance:

By length of toil a bright perfection knew,

Correctly bold, and just in all she drew.

'Till late Corneille, with †Lucan's spirit fir'd,

Breath'd the free strain, as Rome and He inspir'd:

And classic Judgment gain'd to sweet Racine

The temperate strength of Maro's chaster line.

But wilder far the British laurel spread,

And wreaths less artful crown our poet's head.

* About the time of Shakspeare, the poet Hardy was in great repute in France. He wrote, according to Fontenelle, six hundred plays. The French poets after him applied themselves in general to the correct improvement of the stage, which was almost totally disregarded by those of our own country, Jonson excepted.

† The favourite author of the elder Corneille.

Yet he alone to every scene could give

Th' historian's truth, and bid the manners live.

Wak'd at his call, I view with glad surprise,

Majestic forms of mighty monarchs rise.

There Henry's trumpets spread their loud alarms,

And laurell'd Conquest waits her hero's arms.

Here gentler Edward claims a pitying sigh,

Scarce born to honours, and so soon to die!

Yet shall thy throne, unhappy infant! bring

No beam of comfort to the guilty king:

The * time shall come, when Glo'ster's heart shall

    bleed,

In life's last hours, with horror of the deed:

When dreary visions shall at last present

Thy vengeful image in the midnight tent:

* Tempus erit Turno, magno cùm optaverit emptum
Intactum pallanta, &c.

Thy hand unseen the secret death shall bear,

Blunt the weak sword, and break th' oppressive spear.

  Where'er we turn, by Fancy charm'd, we find

Some sweet illusion of the cheated mind.

Oft, wild of wing, she calls the soul to rove

With humbler nature in the rural grove ;

Where swains contented own the quiet scene,

And twilight fairies tread the circled green :

Dress'd by her hand the woods and vallies smile,

And Spring diffusive, decks th' inchanted isle.

  O more than all in powerful genius blest,

Come, take thine empire o'er the willing breast !

Whate'er the wounds this youthful heart shall feel,

Thy songs support me, and thy morals heal !

There every thought the poet's warmth may raise,

There native music dwells in all the lays.

Oh, might some verse with happiest skill persuade

Expressive Picture to adopt thine aid !

What wondrous draughts might rise from every page !

What other Raphaels charm a distant age !

Methinks even now I view some free design,

Where breathing Nature lives in every line :

Chaste and subdued the modest lights decay,

Steal into shades, and mildly melt away.

—And see, where * Anthony, in tears approv'd,

Guards the pale relics of the chief he lov'd :

O'er the old corse the warrior seems to bend,

Deep sunk in grief, and mourns his murder'd friend !

* See the Tragedy of Julius Cæsar.

Still as they press he calls on all around,

Lifts the torn robe, and points the bleeding wound.

But * who is he, whose brows exalted bear

A wrath impatient, and a fiercer air?

Awake to all that injur'd worth can feel,

On his own Rome he turns th' avenging steel.

Yet shall not war's insatiate fury fall,

(So Heaven ordains it) on the destin'd wall.

See the fond mother, 'midst the plaintive train,

Hung on his knees, and prostrate on the plain!

Touch'd to the soul, in vain he strives to hide

The son's affection, in the Roman's pride:

O'er all the man conflicting passions rise,

Rage grasps the sword, while Pity melts the eyes.

* Coriolanus. See Mr. Spence's dialogue on the Odyssey.

Thus, generous Critic, as thy bard inspires,

The sister Arts shall nurse their drooping fires ;

Each from his scenes her stores alternate bring,

Blend the fair tints, or wake the vocal string :

Those Sibyl-leaves, the sport of every wind,

(For poets ever were a careless kind)

By thee dispos'd, no farther toil demand,

But, just to Nature, own thy forming hand.

So spread o'er Greece, th' harmonious whole
    unknown,

Even Homer's numbers charm'd by parts alone.

Their own Ulysses scarce had wander'd more,

By winds and waters cast on every shore :

When rais'd by fate, some former Hanmer join'd

Each beauteous image of the boundless mind ;

And bade, like thee, his Athens ever claim

A fond alliance with the Poet's name.

D I R G E

IN CYMBELINE.

SUNG BY GUIDERUS AND ARVIRAGUS OVER FIDELLE, SUPPOSED TO BE DEAD.

To fair Fidelle's grassy tomb

    Soft maids and village hinds shall bring

Each opening sweet, of earliest bloom,

    And rifle all the breathing Spring.

No wailing ghost shall dare appear

    To vex with shrieks this quiet grove,

But shepherd lads assemble here,

    And melting virgins own their love.

No wither'd witch shall here be seen,

    No goblins lead their nightly crew ;

The female fays shall haunt the green,

    And dress thy grave with pearly dew ;

The red-breast oft at evening hours

    Shall kindly lend his little aid,

With hoary moss, and gather'd flowers,

    To deck the ground where thou art laid.

When howling winds, and beating rain,

    In tempests shake the sylvan cell;

Or 'midst the chase on every plain,

    The tender thought on thee shall dwell.

Each lonely scene shall thee restore,

For thee the tear be duly shed ;

Belov'd, till life can charm no more ;

And mourn'd, till Pity's self be dead.

ODE

ON THE

DEATH OF MR. THOMPSON.

THE SCENE OF THE FOLLOWING STANZAS IS
SUPPOSED TO LIE ON THE THAMES,
NEAR RICHMOND.

I.

IN yonder grave a Druid lies

    Where slowly winds the stealing wave!

The year's best sweets shall duteous rise

    To **deck its** Poet's sylvan grave!

II.

In yon deep bed of whisp'ring reeds

    His airy harp* shall now be laid,

That he, whose heart in sorrow bleeds,

    May love thro' life the soothing shade.

* The harp of ÆOLUS, of which see a description in the
CASTLE OF INDOLENCE.

III.

Then maids and youths shall linger here,

And while its sounds at distance swell,

Shall sadly seem in Pity's ear,

To hear the Woodland Pilgrim's knell.

IV.

Remembrance oft shall haunt the shore

When Thames in summer wreaths is drest,

And oft suspend the dashing oar

To bid his gentle spirit rest!

V.

And oft as Ease and Health retire

To breezy lawn, or forest deep,

The friend shall view yon whitening* spire,

And 'mid the varied landscape weep.

*RICHMOND Church.

·VI.

But Thou, who own'st that earthly bed,

  Ah ! what will every dirge avail ?

Or tears which Love and Pity shed,

   That mourn beneath the gliding sail !

VII.

Yet lives there one, whose heedless eye

   Shall scorn thy pale shrine glimm'ring near ;

With him, sweet bard, may Fancy die,

   And Joy desert the blooming year.

V·III.

But thou, lorn stream, whose sullen tide

   No sedge-crown'd Sisters now attend,

Now waft me from the green hill's side

   Whose cold turf hides the buried friend !

IX.

And see, the fairy valleys fade,

Dun Night has veil'd the solemn view !

Yet once again, dear parted shade,

Meek Nature's child, again adieu !

X.

* The genial meads assign'd to bless

Thy life, shall mourn thy early doom !

Their hinds, and shepherd girls shall dress

With simple hands thy rural tomb.

XI.

Long, long, thy stone, and pointed clay

Shall melt the musing Briton's eyes,

O vales, and wild woods ! shall He say,

In yonder grave Your Druid lies !

---

* Mr. Thomson resided in the neighbourhood of Richmond some time before his death.

AN

O D E

ON THE

POPULAR SUPERSTITIONS

OF THE

HIGHLANDS OF SCOTLAND.

HOME, thou return'st from Thames, whose Naiads

    long

  Have seen thee ling'ring with a fond delay,

  'Mid those soft friends, whose hearts some future day

Shall melt, perhaps, to hear thy tragic song.

Go not unmindful of that cordial youth *,

  Whom, long endear'd, thou leav'st by Lavant's side;

Together let us wish him lasting truth,

  And joy untainted with his destin'd bride.

  * A gentleman of the name of Barrow, who introduced Home

to Collins.

Go : nor regardless, while these numbers boast

    My short-liv'd bliss, forget my social name;

But think, far off, how, on the Southern coast,

    I met thy friendship with an equal flame!

Fresh to that soil thou turn'st, where ev'ry vale

    Shall prompt the poet, and his song demand :

To thee thy copious subjects ne'er shall fail;

    Thou need'st but take thy pencil to thy hand,

    And paint what all believe, who own thy genial

      land.

II.

There must thou wake perforce thy Doric quill;

    'Tis Fancy's land to which thou sett'st thy feet;

    Where still, 'tis said, the Fairy people meet,

Beneath each birken shade, or mead or hill.

There each trim lass, that skims the milky store

    To the swart tribes, their creamy bowls allots ;

By night they sip it round the cottage-door,

    While airy minstrels warble jocund notes.

There, ev'ry herd, by sad experience, knows

    How, wing'd with Fate, their elf-shot arrows fly,

When the sick ewe her summer food foregoes,

    Or, stretch'd on earth, the heart-smit heifers lie.

Such airy beings awe the untutor'd swain :

    Nor thou, tho' learn'd, his homelier thoughts

        neglect ;

Let thy sweet Muse the rural faith sustain ;

    These are the themes of simple, sure effect,

That add new conquests to her boundless reign,

And fill, with double force, her heart-commanding

        strain.

III.

Ev'n yet preserv'd, how often may'st thou hear,

    Where to the pole the Boreal mountains run,

    Taught by the father, to his list'ning son,

Strange lays, whose pow'r had charm'd a Spenser's ear.

At ev'ry pause, before thy mind possest,

    Old Runic bards shall seem to rise around, —

With uncouth lyres, in many-colour'd vest,

    Their matted hair with boughs fantastic crown'd:

Whether thou bid'st the well-taught hind repeat

    The choral dirge that mourns some chieftain brave,

When ev'ry shrieking maid her bosom beat,

    And strew'd with choicest herbs his scented grave;

Or whether, sitting in the shepherd's shiel *,

    Thou hear'st some sounding tale of war's alarms;

When at the bugle's call, with fire and steel,

---

* A summer hut, built in the high part of the mountains, to
tend their flocks in the warm season, when the pasture is fine.

The sturdy clans pour'd forth their brawny swarms,

And hostile brothers met to prove each others arms.

IV.

'Tis thine to sing, how, framing hideous spells,

  In Sky's lone isle, the gifted wizard-seer,

  Lodg'd in the wintry cave, with Fate's fell spear;

Or in the depth of Uist's dark forest dwells:

  How they, whose sight such dreary dreams engross,

With their own vision oft astonish'd droop,

  When o'er the watry strath or quaggy moss,

They see the gliding ghosts unbodied troop.

  Or, if in sports, or on the festive green,

Their destin'd glance some fated youth descry,

  Who now, perhaps, in lusty vigour seen,

And rosy health, shall soon lamented die.

For them the viewless forms of air obey;

Their bidding heed, and at their beck repair.

They know what spirit brews the stormful day,

And heartless, oft like moody madness, stare

To see the phantom train their secret work prepare.

V.

" Or on some bellying rock that shades the deep,

  " They view the lurid signs that cross the sky,

  " Where, in the west, the brooding tempests lie;

" And hear their first, faint, rustling pennons sweep.

" **Or** in the archèd cave, where deep and dark

  " The broad, unbroken billows heave and swell,

" In horrid musings rapt, they sit to mark

  " The lab'ring moon; or list the nightly yell

I

" Of that dread spirit, whose gigantic form

   " The seer's entranced eye can well survey,

" Thro' the dim air who guides the driving storm,

   " And points the wretched bark its destin'd prey.

" Or him who hovers on his flagging wing,

   " O'er the dire whirlpool, that, in ocean's waste,

" Draws instant down whate'er devoted thing

   " The failing breeze within its reach hath plac'd—

   " The distant seaman hears, and flies with trembling

     " haste.

VI.

   " Or, if on land the fiend exerts his sway,

" Silent he broods o'er quicksand, bog or fen,

   " Far from the shelt'ring roof and haunts of men,

" When **witched** darkness shuts the eye of **day,**

" And shrouds each star that wont to cheer the

" night ;

" Or, if the drifted snow perplex the way,

" With treach'rous gleam he lures the fated wight,

" And leads him flound'ring on and quite astray."

VII.

Ah, luckless swain ! o'er all unblest, indeed !

Whom late bewilder'd in the dank, dark fen,

Far from his flocks, and smoking hamlet, then !

To that **sad** spot where hums the sedgy weed :

On him, enrag'd, the fiend, in angry **mood,**

Shall never look with pity's kind concern,

But instant, furious, raise the whelming flood

O'er its drown'd banks, forbidding all return !.

Or, if he meditate his wish'd escape,

To some dim hill that seems uprising near,

   To his faint eye, the grim and grisly shape,

In all its terrors clad, shall wild appear.

   Mean time the wat'ry surge shall round him rise,

Pour'd sudden forth from ev'ry swelling source!

— What now remains but tears and hopeless sighs?

His fear-shook limbs have lost their youthly force,

And down the waves he floats, a pale and breathless

    corse!

VIII.

For him in vain his anxious wife shall wait,

   Or wander forth to meet him on his way;

   For him in vain at to-fall of the day,

His babes shall linger at th' unclosing gate!

Ah, ne'er shall he return ! Alone, if night,

   Her travell'd limbs in broken slumbers steep !

With drooping willows drest, his mournful sprite

   Shall visage sad, perchance, her silent sleep :

Then he, perhaps, with moist and wat'ry hand

   Shall fondly seem to press her shudd'ring cheek,

And with his blue-swoln face before her stand,

   And, shiv'ring cold, these piteous accents speak :

" Pursue, dear wife ! thy daily toils pursue,

   " At dawn or dusk, industrious as before ;

" Nor e'er of me one helpless thought renew,

   " While I lie welt'ring on the osier'd shore,

   " Drown'd by the Kelpie's* wrath, nor e'er shall

    aid thee more !"

* The water fiend.

IX.

Unbounded is thy range; with varied skill

    Thy Muse may, like those feath'ry tribes which spring

    From their rude rocks, extend her skirting wing

Round the moist marge of each cold Hebrid isle,

    To that hoar pile * which still its ruin shows :

In whose small vaults a pigmy-folk is found,

    Whose bones the delver with his spade upthrows,

And culls them, wond'ring, from the hallow'd ground !

  Or thither †, where beneath the show'ry west,

    The mighty kings of three fair realms are laid :

Once foes, perhaps, together now they rest,

    No slaves revere them, and no wars invade :

---

* One of the Hebrides is called The Isle of Pigmies, where it
is reported, that several miniature bones of the human species
have been dug **up in** the ruins of the chapel **there.**

  † Icolmkill, one of the Hebrides, where near sixty of the ancient Scottish, Irish, and Norwegian kings are interred.

Yet frequent now, at midnight solemn hour,

  The rifted mounds their yawning cells unfold,

And forth the monarchs stalk with sov'reign pow'r,

  In pageant robes ; and, wreath'd with sheeny gold,

  And on their twilight tombs aërial council hold.

X.

But, oh ! o'er all, forget not Kilda's race,

  On whose bleak rocks, which brave the wasting

    tides,

  Fair Nature's daughter, Virtue, yet abides.

Go ! just, as they, their blameless manners trace !

  Then to my ear transmit some gentle song,

Of those whose lives are yet sincere and plain,

  Their bounded walks the rugged cliffs along,

And all their prospect but the wintry main.

With sparing temp'rance at the needful time,

They drain the scented spring; or, hunger-prest,

  Along th' Atlantic rock, undreading, climb,

And of its eggs despoil the Solan's * nest.

  Thus, blest in primal innocence they live,

Suffic'd, and happy with that frugal fare

  Which tasteful toil and hourly danger give.

Hard is their shallow soil, and bleak and bare;

Nor ever vernal bee was heard to murmur there!

XI.

Nor need'st thou blush that such false themes engage

  Thy gentle mind, of fairer stores possest;

  For not alone they touch the village breast,

But fill'd in elder time, th' historic page.

---

* An aquatic bird, on the eggs of which the inhabitants of St. Kilda, another of the Hebrides, chiefly fubsist

There, Shakspeare's self, with ev'ry garland

   crown'd,

Flew to those fairy climes his fancy sheen,

  In musing hour; his wayward sisters found,

And with their terrors drest the magic scene.

  From them he sung, when, 'mid his bold design,

Before the Scot, afflicted, and aghast !

  The shadowy kings of Banquo's fated line,

Thro' the dark cave in gleamy pageant past.

  Proceed ! nor quit the tales which, simply told,

Could once so well my answ'ring bosom pierce;

  Proceed, in forceful sounds, and colour bold,

The native legends of thy land rehearse ;

To such adapt thy lyre, and suit thy powerful verse.

XII.

In scenes like these, which, daring to depart

From sober truth, are still to Nature true,

And call forth fresh delight to Fancy's view,

Th' heroic Muse employ'd her Tasso's art !

— How have I trembled, when at Tancred's stroke,

Its gushing blood the gaping cypress pour'd !

When each live plant with mortal accents spoke,

And the wild blast upheav'd the vanish'd sword !

How have I sat, when pip'd the pensive wind,

To hear his harp by British Fairfax strung !

Prevailing poet ! whose undoubting mind,

Believ'd the magic wonders which he sung !

Hence, at each sound, imagination glows !

Hence, at each picture, vivid life starts here!

Hence his warm lay with softest sweetness flows!

Melting it flows, pure, murm'ring, strong and clear,

And fills th'impassion'd heart, and wins th' harmo-

nious ear!

XIII.

All hail! ye scenes, **that** o'er my soul prevail!

Ye splendid friths and lakes, which, far away,

Are by smooth Annan * fill'd, or past'ral Tay †,

Or Don's ‡ romantic springs, at distance, **hail**!

The time shall come, when I, perhaps, may tread

Your lowly glens, o'erhung with spreading broom;

Or o'er your stretching heaths, by Fancy led;

Or o'er your mountains creep in awful gloom!

* † ‡ Three rivers in Scotland.

Then will I dress once more the faded bower,

   Where Jonson * sat in Drummond's classic shade;

Or crop, from Tiviotdale, each lyric flower,

   And mourn, on Yarrow's banks, where Willy's laid !

Mean time, ye pow'rs **that** on the plains which bore

   The cordial youth, on Lothian's plains, attend!—

Where'er Home dwells, on hill, or lowly moor,

   To him I lose, your kind protection lend,

   And, touch'd with love like mine, preserve my

      absent friend !

* Ben Jonson paid a visit on foot, in 1619, to the Scotch poet Drummond, **at his seat of Hawthornden, within four** miles **of** Edinburgh.

THE END.

www.ingramcontent.com/pod-product-compliance
Lightning Source LLC
Chambersburg PA
CBHW030610040726

47497CB00008B/2928